For Mangaliso

"I'm yet to find a definitive answer to any question worth asking."

—Miguel Mbele

1 THE DM

"Hei"—that would be it. He didn't know what else to write at first, but after some thought he concluded that over such a superficial medium his first words would not have the capacity to make her reply if she didn't like his profile pictures. Whereas, if chosen incorrectly, his first words might actually have the irreparable effect of putting her off, irrespective of his profile. So he settled for the timeless 'hello' but in her native language, thinking that this subtle variation, given his distinctly non-Finnish name and look, might prove catching enough to make her browse his profile.

On his profile: it was a meticulously curated collection of pics, clips, and gifs highlighting all his best qualities—his abs, his tallness, his fashion style, and his photography. What he didn't fail to realise is that, in the process, he was also alluding to one of his most negative qualities, for only an internally insecure person would try so hard to have such a perfect profile. But this didn't bother him too much, because he estimated that the majority of women would not be so attentive and perceptive as to pick up on this from his profile or even from the first date, and these would be exactly the ones he would attempt to sleep with on the second.

On sleeping with women on the second date: this was merely a compromise because most of the women he dated held strong reservations against having sex on the first

1

night. (He never directly discussed it with them, but he reckoned that a combination of social norms, biological factors, and his emotional unavailability formed the basis of their reservations.) Of course, he would have much preferred to have sex on the first night; however, the reasons for this were often misunderstood by his peers. It wasn't because he could have sex with more women that way.[1] No, it was because he considered himself a good judge of character and a man who knew exactly what he wanted. As such, he always knew what he wanted to do with a woman after a glimpse of her face, a scan of her physique, a taste of her aroma, and the third conversation topic. And given his remarkable ability to flip through topics, he could usually make up his mind—full steam ahead versus emergency break—by the thirtieth minute of any first date.

He'd had a feeling that this first date with Elsa would not follow the usual script. He rationalised this emotion as his hope of her being partial to having sex on the first night. And he predicated this aspiration on the socially progressive reputation that precedes her Nordic culture. But it's more likely that what he was really experiencing was a primal sense of excitement (aka butterflies) for the first time in a long time.

Elsa had a beautiful sharp face and almost mysteriously smelled of Coco Mademoiselle, his all-time favourite. But she wore loose-fitting clothes—monochrome black with angular lines—making it next to impossible for him to judge

---

[1] That logic is actually fallacious, but we had better save that conversation for another time.

her physique. Furthermore, she managed to completely control the conversation, probing carefully, listening analytically, giving away little about herself without seeming guarded, and only allowing the topic to change once she felt she'd dug deep enough. She didn't even let him perform his stock evasive manoeuvres: when he suddenly called a timeout to go to the toilet then returned with a funny story to share, she swiftly went back to where they'd left off as soon as he was finished with his story. And so after two hours, three courses, and four wine glasses, he still had no idea of what he wanted to do with Elsa—but he desperately wanted to find out.

Back at his living room, listening to Radiohead and drinking Bourbon now, he sat in his favourite chair facing the window. The living city lights outside were fighting the reflection of a single tungsten lamp for his attention, both losing out to the visions echoing in his mind. Images of her form would flash suddenly and decay slowly, lingering with viscosity and combining with the sweet-spicy Kentucky aftertaste to create a new kind of whiskey altogether. The corners of her mouth as they gave birth to her smile, the tendons in her neck as they held her head at varying angles, the hypnotic dance between her thumb and index finger as they spun her spaghetti... Continuing in this manner, consciousness escaped him, and he drifted off into an amber sleep. (The fact that he had begun to fall in love had also escaped him.)

2 THE BIRTHDAY PARTY

Their second encounter was preceded by a week of pervasive anticipation, ranging from mild to intense but always present. Several times he'd messaged her and been left waiting for her reply, and several times he'd been left wondering what her reply actually meant. When Elsa eventually committed to seeing him again, he was thrilled. And while he couldn't deny his excitement, he conveniently put it down to a sense of satisfaction from his mastery of The Game.

But his satisfaction was short-lived because a few hours after his "Be there like a Teddy bear!" reply to her "Are you free this Friday night for some food and drinks?" message, he received another: "Feel free to bring a +1." He considered getting angry at her—he wondered if he ought to feel stupid for having got his hopes so high and thus if he ought to blame her for his innocent misunderstanding of her ambiguous invitation—but he decided not to. Instead, he brushed it aside and attempted to get on with some work. But he struggled with an unusually dry throat, so he popped out of his photography studio and walked across the street to get himself an iced coffee.

It wasn't until the day of their second encounter—deliberating over three different outfits spread out on his bed, rehearsing mini-speeches that he would give as answers to the inevitable 'So how do you know Elsa?' and

4

'What do you do for a living?' and debating whether his earlier decision not to take a wingman had been really brave or rather foolish—that he began to question his commitment to winning her over. All of a sudden he felt an inexplicable, almost uncontrollable urge to cancel.

His mind was harkened back to his childhood when, on the morning of the first Monday of every July, on the dawn of the day he was due to depart for summer camp, he would cry and beg his mother not to send him away. His pleas would be met with her leather slipper to his face. And so with swollen eyes and bruised cheeks he would solemnly board the coach, only to return two weeks later with new songs, jokes, and tricks to show his mum, dad, and sister.

Heeding these childhood lessons, he ignored his reluctance to go to the party, had a self-deprecating inner monologue, and ploughed forward with the preparations. He picked his safest outfit, the one that would elicit the least controversy, a black-on-black combo by ALYX; and his favourite cologne, the one that would arouse the most desire, La Nuit by YSL. Then he masturbated over a POV handjob video with a very talkative woman, after which he jumped in the shower and masturbated again, visualising a similar scene but this time with Elsa doing the manual labour while taking directions from the talkative woman who was right by her side commentating and supplying spit for lubrication—and for visual effect.

He continued with the shower: he exfoliated, rinsed, cleansed, rinsed, oiled, and rinsed—in that order. He got out and brushed his teeth without a towel. He put on MJ's Off The Wall and continued to air-dry while singing and grooving to it. He very delicately patted himself dry to Human Nature. He got dressed to I Wanna Be Startin'

Somethin'. Then he wrapped up his preparations—put on his jacket, stuffed the usual belongings inside it, and grabbed his rucksack with his bottle for the party—to The Girl is Mine ft. Paul McCartney. He closed the door, locked it, then stood on his doormat for a brief moment redirecting his iPhone's music from his Sonos to his AirPods. Once he had P.Y.T. in his ears, he spun 540° then grabbed his crotch to lift himself into a toe stand before skipping past the front lawn while clicking his fingers and nodding his head to the gratifying beat. As soon as he turned the corner of his street into Elgin Avenue and into the golden-hour sun, he took a selfie to check, one last time, how good he looked. "I look fucking amazing," he thought, "handsome, presentable, almost wholesome!" So he forwarded the picture to several girls—but obviously not to Elsa.

He didn't jump on the 18 bus or call an Uber; he walked to the party. The address wasn't far and the weather wasn't bad, but mostly he was worried about not turning up late enough. In a perfect world, he would have liked to arrive one minute after the second guest and about twenty minutes before the fourth. But in this uncertain world, he couldn't risk coming across as an eager beaver, especially after the feel-free-to-bring-a-plus-one fiasco. Plus he was concerned about her friends not approving of him. So he aimed his arrival for when the core guests would be loosened up after a few drinks and most receptive to him, the outsider to the group.

His Google Maps told him he was nearing his destination. In reminding himself of all he had going for him, he felt particularly positive about his drink decision. "Drinking whiskey makes a man more attractive," he thought, "but only if he can speak about it critically and confidently, otherwise he is no more attractive than a man chugging cheap cider." And not only could he talk about his chosen whiskey, The Quiet Man, critically and confidently from a gustatory perspective, but he also had a charming anecdote of how he first came across this boutique, single malt Irish.

When he arrived at his destination, he took a second to examine where she lived: a small gated development of two-story art and design studios in an otherwise mostly residential street near Kensal Rise. When he entered the compound, this is what he noticed (in chronological order): one, the gate closed behind him too slowly leaving a window of opportunity for an intruder to slip in unnoticed; two, the security cameras covering the courtyard were highly visible and had a large blind spot; and three, quail-egg pebbles on the driveway were within dangerous proximity to the studio's floor-to-ceiling glass walls. (His risk awareness was a talent he'd cultivated from an early age, initially by playing GoldenEye on his N64 and Metal Gear Solid on his neighbour's PS.) Security vulnerabilities uncovered, he continued to scan the exterior in search of insights into her life. There were four statues of cats lining the walkways to each studio. These guardians had LED eyes guiding visitors' feet along black granite. And the doorbell was seemingly made out of a large opaque glass marble. It was cold and smooth to the touch, just like the ones he worshipped—as in, actually prayed to—as a kid.

Most of these observations would prove to be successful conversation starters at the party, especially the LED cats. Unfortunately, they would add nothing to his understanding of Elsa, because not only did she not live there, but it was also her first time seeing the place. As he later discovered, the task of sorting out this venue, indeed of organising the entire party, had been eagerly taken up by her good friend and flatmate Maria. He smirked on the inside at the speed at which he, one, recognised what a strategically important person this Maria was and, two, came up with a plan of attack.

The studio was full of people too drunk to notice his arrival, there was '70s Funk being blasted out of powerful speakers by a semi-professional DJ, and there were several chafing dishes full of rice and Thai green curry—his favourite. All of this pleased him. But everyone was drinking from either a pony keg of larger that Maria had bought or a jumbo pitcher of sangria that Maria had made, and he worried that he might stand out—and not in a good way—if he were to be seen drinking something different, so he made a judgement call and decided not to take his bottle of whiskey out of his rucksack.

Around ninety minutes and a similar number of beer sips into the party, and not wanting to waste a whiskey backstory whose charm had been empirically proven on countless occasions, he had the idea of presenting The Quiet Man to Elsa as a gift. But when he tried to give her the bottle she politely rejected. And when he insisted she resisted. So, to end the stalemate, he put it back in his rucksack and put on a brave face and told her he would save it for their next date. Immediately following this brief exchange, he began to feel vertigo, blood pressing against his face, and vomit rising up his throat. Ashamed, he hurried to the toilet to piss out some of the beer and drink water from the tap without being seen.

After recuperating from that rejection and embarrassing

near-accident, he refocused his efforts on his main line of attack: impressing Maria. He approached this endeavour with the expectation that she would feedback to Elsa what an interesting/funny/good guy he was—either accolade would be fine. That was the plan; it seemed simple enough, but the execution would be more challenging. He needed to impress Maria, but he couldn't do it directly nor blatantly because that might backfire.

He found an opening! He saw Maria on the terrace talking to a man and woman that looked like a happily married couple. Good![2] He approached them by moving in a way that would not reveal his destination, let alone his intention. They just so happened to be talking about rape and sexual assault in light of the #MeToo movement. Perfect! He dived straight in without a moment's hesitation because he'd recently attended an interpretative dance performance on sexual assault which had sparked some pretty interesting ideas in him. (Actually, there was a little more to it than that: he'd jotted down some notes during the performance with the intention of sharing them in the ensuing Q&A session, but he'd been inexplicably stricken with shyness and had never got a chance to share them, so he'd gone home that evening disappointed in himself and had developed the notes into an essay, of sorts. And now

---

[2] Approaching a small group made up primarily of happy couples in secure relationships is a safe bet—less chance of bumping heads with territorial single men or defensive single women, and almost no risk of being ganged up against should the discussion intensify (since a steady couple can always be turned against each other humorously easily).

here he was, finally getting a chance to air it!)

"You know I actually think that a lot of the discourse that's trending on social media—most of it by well-intentioned, progressively minded individuals—is anti-feminist," he said by way of introduction. He looked at the man but focused on Maria's attention which he could sense he now had in full. The big opening had worked. He turned his glance to the woman. "Centuries ago, laws written by powerful men to create and enforce a society in their image, embedded in our legal system a patriarchal bias. But where do we stand nowadays? Nowadays we, as an imperfect society; we, trying to be equitable while still very much biased; we, empty in understanding but seeking enlightenment; we are working hard to address the residual imbalance and attain a moral reparation. But we are doing it by recognising our male flaws and not by recognising our female strengths and virtues." He finally added Maria to his game of alternating glances. "For example, where does the belief come from that it is men that need to gain consent from women?" He was particularly proud of how provocatively he'd phrased this question. "As in, why do we still assume that it's men who will initiate the sexual encounter?" He paused to allow his rhetorical questions to sink in but continued before any of his listeners could interject: "Eradicating rape culture is, of course and without a doubt, of critical importance. But I'm presently disenchanted with any discourse that's premised on the reductionist dichotomy of men as powerful predators and women as vulnerable victims. Granted, we are the inheritors of a society where this was overwhelmingly the case, so I'm incredibly relieved that it's finally being recognised in our legal system and in the realm of public opinion. But retrospective recognition is only the first step towards lasting change and now we must continue to push forward... I fear that by emphasising consent to such an extent, by pushing it until it becomes the number-one-trending feminism topic on social media, we may be retrograding and distracting our focus from the bigger picture. I think that pressure groups, campaigners, policymakers, and all the rest of us need to move beyond a reparative agenda towards more progressive ideals. Our ambitions ought to be much more aspirational. They ought to emancipate our notion of Woman to that of a full human being with sexual and other desires as rampant or as placid as that of any man. That, in my opinion, is the true essence of feminism. Therefore, as feminists," he said pre-emptively to trap them into agreement, "we should never let ourselves be distracted by weak substitutes, regardless of how well-intentioned they may be. Again, of course, always fully cognizant of the gravity of sexual harassment and sexual assault and rape."

"Very impressive!" said the woman after she felt secure that he'd finished. Emboldened by her response, her partner actually clapped a few times before awkwardly trying to style it out like he'd been rubbing something stubborn off his hands. Thankfully, Maria saved them all from this super cringe moment. "Interesting views," she said concealing a faint smile. "Come with me to get a drink?" He nodded to the embarrassed couple as a farewell bid then followed her inside.

By the sangria bucket, Maria explained the reason for pulling him away. He would step out first; she would follow shortly after. They would take the strawberry gateau out of the boot of the car, set the candles, and light them. She would go back inside, kill the lights, and start the singing. This would be his prompt to deliver the cake to Elsa before—and she couldn't stress this enough—before the song's end.

He didn't like this last part of the plan. He thought the position of cake bearer carried too much responsibility. She didn't like his trepidation. He clarified that he wasn't scared of dropping the cake, but that the cake bearer should be someone closer to Elsa. Maria accepted his feedback and switched their roles.

In the end, her plan was executed beautifully. And over the following days, the Facebook video of Elsa making a silent wish and blowing out twenty-nine candles would be liked and commented on by dozens of people.

Riding the cab home, feeling like he'd just won a prize, he put a stop to a nascent smile as soon as he noticed it being propagated across the quiet cabin and on to the driver's empathetic face. He suddenly felt betrayed by his defence mechanisms for not protecting him as they usually did. Why should he be so happy? He hadn't even got a kiss from Elsa. He should have been her birthday present. He should have fucked her until she multiple-orgasmed. Instead, here he was, falling asleep to the soft whirl of an electric motor and the soporific murmur of rolling tires on tarmac.

3 THE DREAM

"October is the most romantic month of the year in London," is what he thought to himself as he stepped outside his house that Sunday morning. The seasons were changing, the grey sky above him was pierced by the semi-naked branches of trees of a genus completely unknown to him, and the fallen beech leaves—some were blonde like Elsa's hair, while some were as red as blood itself. "What a shame it is that dry leaves don't stain the pavement when you step on them." He carried on crunching them as he walked, trying to spot a pattern between the colour and the sound.

He came back with the raw chestnuts he'd gone out for and went straight into the kitchen to pre-heat the oven to 200°C. Using a paring knife, he made careful incisions on each of the twenty chestnuts he'd selected to form his portion. He put them in a roasting tin in the oven then set the timer for 20min. He went up the flight of stairs to his room to change back into his super comfortable pyjamas and to grab his weed. Sunday was his favourite day of the week.

When he returned to the kitchen he looked out to the patio and saw that it had begun to rain softly. Soft rain made him feel uneasy. Dry weather made him feel at ease, as did heavy downpours, but not this English drizzle. To fight this sensation, he rushed to the storage closet under the stairs to grab his wellies and an umbrella then stepped out into the kitchen patio to stand under the trickling rain in defiance. With squinted eyes, he tilted his head slightly to take a closer look at the marijuana burning gladly inside the bowl of his aluminium pipe and felt a gush of gratitude towards his dealer for the reliable supply of his magical herbs.

Once he finished smoking his pipe, he stepped inside and began making a chai tea. He sat staring at the flames on the stove which were trying to pierce the bottom of an old-style kettle. They looked like twelve fangs. He thought it would be cool to have a necklace made out of incandescent fangs. He imagined himself naked on an empty beach at night wearing his incandescent fang necklace, walking towards Elsa, being trailed by a pack of guardian LED cats.

The kettle whistled at him. He placed a ring made out of his index finger and thumb between his lips and whistled back. As he finished pouring the tea into his thermos, the oven timer rang. He peeled one chestnut: it was done. He placed the rest of them in a newspaper cone then moved to the living room.

He ate all twenty chestnuts and drank most of the tea in the thermos before falling asleep on the living room couch halfway through Harsh Times. He'd seen that film in its entirety at least ten times but had started it at least fifty. These forty-odd dreams had all been vivid—usually violent, sometimes carnal—but this nap introduced a whole new set of imagery.

An hour or so later, Hugo—his dealer, landlord, and housemate—returned home and went to wake him up but didn't get a chance to.

"Wake! Wake! Wake!" erupted from the sleeping man,

his retinas scanning the inside of his eyelids as if searching for a way out of his slumber.

"What?" replied Hugo, giggling at the impeccable irony of the timing.

"Hugo?" He was still lying down but his eyes were now half-opened.

"Yes, it's me."

His eyes fanned out to capture his surroundings a split second before his nostrils flared to take in a rush of air. The sharpness of his inhale created the illusion that his torso had been lifted by the air pressure differential. "Shit, bro, when did you get here?"

"Bro, I got here just now. You fell asleep with the stove on, so I tried to wake you up to make sure you were alright."

"Shit, I must've forgotten to turn it off after I made my tea. Did you—"

"Yeah, I turned it off already."

"Safe."

"Bro, your first words when you woke up were kind of funny though. What were you dreaming about?"

"You must have heard me trying to wake him up... Shit, it was a mindfuck of a dream. I don't know if any of it will make any sense."

"Well, let's see. Start from the beginning."

He paused to collect his thoughts. The strangeness of the sequence of events he was about to describe quickly dawned on him. He kissed his teeth. "You know what? It's probably not gonna make sense whichever way I tell it, so fuck it. I was in the zoo, but it was like a human zoo with all types of humans in these small enclosures behind a two-way mirror. They had live humans from all sorts of civilisations—past and present—from prehistoric cave dwellers to like, current-day Eskimos and shit. I was walking holding hands with my dad. Only he was younger than me. He was a child of about... well, age makes no sense here. But he was roughly half my height and I was his guardian and I was looking after him but somehow he kept shrinking, getting smaller and smaller until his little hand slipped out of mine and I could no longer grab it because he was too low. I kneeled down to scoop him up and put him in my pocket but I misjudged the motion and he fell onto the floor and rolled through the slits of a gutter into the sewer. I started crying. I could see him trapped behind the metal bars but I couldn't get him out. I kept fucking crying and crying and before I knew it the tears were forming a stream and flowing into the gutter. My father was holding on to the bars until he lost his strength and was swept away by the river that I had cried."

"Fuck!"

"Yeah..." He heaved a deep sigh and repositioned himself. "But then a woman, a park ranger—I don't know when but the human zoo had somehow transformed into an empty safari—she picked me up from the foetal position that I had assumed underneath a sole pink cherry blossom in the middle of a limitless prairie and told me that she had found my father."

"Sakura... That's interesting," Hugo thought. "Bro, how do you know what type of tree it was?"

"Er, no idea. I guess she must have told me or let me know somehow. Why?"

"Nothing. Please continue. You say she picked you up?"

"Yeah, I couldn't move. I was frozen by the terror of

what I had done, or rather, what had happened under my watch." He shifted the narration to the present tense and his eyes glazed over as if he were reliving the story under a hypnotic spell. "So this ranger woman picks me up and carries me in her arms to a nearby lab where my father is being kept. The lab is underground, and to enter it she has to carry me down a long flight of stairs where each step is made out of silver metallophone bars. The music of her footsteps balloons until the air is thick with the most ethereal harmony. Then suddenly it stops—we have arrived at the entrance. Ranger woman gently lowers me and I'm again able to stand on my own two feet. Next to the entrance there is a slender wooden pedestal, kind of like a small tree only with ornate carvings on its surface and a single branch at the top protruding horizontally. A brown owl is hanging upside down from this branch like a bat. Without actually talking, using only its eyes, it asks us where we've been. Feeling sorry for myself, I simply say that I've made a terrible mistake. Ranger woman tells the owl that I'm here to see my father. Then the owl's head rotates almost a full circle, and simultaneously the doors to the laboratory slide open as if their opening mechanism were driven by its neck. On the inside there's an all-white atrium marked by a glass fountain with pearls for water. This space is empty yet full of people..." This paradox seemed to trigger an awaking from his trance. His focus oscillated as it reconciled the faraway horizon of his dream with the short distance of his current reality, then his glance fluttered as it frantically searched for meaning in the objects in the room. Only once his stare found Hugo's did his pupils fully recover their normal dilation and his eyes regain their consciousness. "I know it may not make much sense, but that's exactly how it was."

"Dreams aren't meant to be logical, bro. Carry on."

He paused to recollect, then continued: "I'm not sure how, but ranger woman was now a magnificent golden ostrich dragging a long train of beautiful peacock feathers from her tail. She kept repeating 'Just this way!' over and over as she guided me through a set of long and dizzying spiral corridors. Finally, we came to the room where my father was being kept. It was a vast round vault with a concrete-domed roof and no windows. And in its centre, my father was floating inside a massive glass tank full of transparent fluid. He was slowly being grown back to his full size by countless identical scientists in white coats. Their heads were hairless, moist, and without bone structure—kind of like the head of an earthworm. They were hovering aimlessly, mumbling inaudibly, twitching incessantly. They couldn't see or hear us, or maybe they simply didn't want to acknowledge us. The golden ostrich asked me if I wanted her to wake up my father. I wondered whether that might impede his regeneration, but I found myself nodding because I was eager to hold him again. Her tail feathers began to rise and spread out like a fan then blowing her chest out she started bellowing 'Wake! Wake! Wake!' in what seemed to be an alien sound frequency. Her all-pervasive voice echoed sonorously through the chamber, louder and louder and louder until I woke up and I saw you."

"Bro, it always amazes me that you can remember your dreams so vividly... Anyway, as you know, normally I wouldn't have interrupted your sleep. But I saw the stove on—and it's not like you to forget such things—and when I smelled the weed—and it seemed like you had smoked a lot of it—I suppose I got a slight case of the dealer's remorse and worried that you had, er, overprescribed yourself some of my magical 'erbs!"

"Nah, I didn't smoke too much, just my usual Sunday-morning pipe. But I don't know, bro. I don't know what's gotten into me. This dream felt a bit more... something than usual." He couldn't find the right word: 'poignant'. He didn't lack the vocabulary just the emotional understanding.

"Listen. Your dream. You know what I'm gonna say next, right?"

"I know. But you know I don't like that psychoanalysis shit."

"But this one was extremely symbolic, so let me just give you some quick thoughts. It won't take but five minutes, bro. And if you don't like the interpretations you can always ignore them."

Hugo went on to expound his psychoanalysis in a detailed but succinct fashion. Indeed the dream was rich with symbolism easily believable without a leap of the imagination or a proclivity for the spiritual. Which is why straight after the analysis, he turned his gaze to Hugo and with an expression of acknowledgement and gratitude said: "I have to go make a phone call."

Hugo was the best dealer, landlord, housemate, and friend he'd ever had. He found it easy to accept the first three, but for him dependency was a sign of weakness and friendship a form of co-dependency. As a child, when his father took a gun to his mouth and pulled the trigger, he lost his closest friend and made a vow never to let himself feel a similar loss again. And on the day he became an adult, when his mother shared some truths about his father that she'd been keeping from him, including the events that led to his suicide, he began to question the existence of love itself.

He left home one minute after his birthday surprise, moved to London two weeks later, and didn't see or speak to his mother for another three years—although she never stopped writing. It wasn't until she was diagnosed with Stage-4 breast cancer that he replied to her. He went back to Madrid and stayed by her side for five months as her sole carer throughout the entire unsuccessful treatment. Six days after her cremation, he boarded a plane to Equatorial Guinea to scatter her ashes in the place of her birth. When the plane's doors opened seven hours later, humid tropical air rushed in and filled the cabin and his lungs. Childhood memories flooded back. Without warning, his eyes also flooded. And within eight heartbeats, his face was wet and his body completely frozen. That was the last time he cried. That was almost nine years ago now.

He never made it outside that airport, and he never scattered his mother's ashes in the place of her birth. He flushed them down the nearest toilet then bought the first ticket back to Madrid. He flew back on the same day, on the same plane, and with the same crew. Amanda, the cabin manager who had talked him through his earlier panic attack, upgraded him free of charge to First Class and closely watched over him while he mostly slept. After landing she asked him if he had anyone to go to, then offered to keep him company since he didn't. They ended up back at her apartment that night. He moved in ten days later.

He was reminded of Amanda just before he called Elsa.

He thought his air hostess would approve of his new love interest, and somehow that gave him confidence. He was laying on his back across his bed with his legs vertical against the wall. This L-shape was his default position for talking on the phone with a girl. He found it extremely comfortable. Also, it made his voice sound husky.

From the first to the last ring, his thoughts raced from "Okay, here we go. Play it cool!" to "I fucking knew it. They're all the fucking same!"—and not as the crow flies. What's more, since she hadn't picked up, he now had to write her a message explaining the unsolicited phone call. "Hey I was just calling to see how you were feeling after the big party. Xx" After a few minutes staring up at the ceiling, wiggling his feet, and wondering what Elsa might be doing, he decided to get up. He bent his knees a little, placed the palms of his feet against the wall, and pushed himself into a reverse cartwheel. He landed on the side of his bed in an upright position, feet together and arms overhead like an Olympic gymnast after the final jump. "You're still a champ!" he told himself. A defiant mood in the face of a minor defeat. He went to the bathroom to brush his teeth, to feel fresh, to get his swagger back. Six-sevenths into it, after brushing top/bottom-front/left/right but before brushing his tongue, his phone rang.

"Hi, Miguel. Sorry I missed your call."

4 THE PHONE CALL

"One sec..." Miguel hastily brushed his tongue then rinsed and dried his mouth. "Okay, I'm with you now."

"You sure? I can call back later if you're busy."

"No, no. I was just in the middle of brushing my teeth, but I'm done now." He headed over to his room.

"Okay."

"What are you up to?"

"Chilling at home. Just finished my weekly skin routine."

"Oh, you have a weekly skin routine?"

"How else do you think I manage to get such beautifully clear and radiant skin on all my selfies? A filter app called FaceTune free from the App Store? Oh please!"

He chuckled.

"You called me earlier."

"I did, yes. I wanted to thank you for the other night."

"Ha! That's what she said."

He cracked up.

"But thank you for coming."

"Aha! That's what she said!"

It was her turn to crack up.

"No, but seriously, thank you for inviting me to your birthday party. I had a great time."

"I'm glad you did. I did too."

"Yeah, you could tell."

"It was just so nice being surrounded by so many of my

friends, you know? Kind of makes me feel like I've gained a second home here in London."

"You have really cool friends."

"Yes!"

"Especially Maria."

"Oh my god, she's the best! I absolutely adore her. Can you imagine all the work she must have put into organising that party all on her own?"

"A lot."

"I wasn't even going to have a party before she got involved! But I'm glad she did. I'm very lucky to have met her. I could never have asked for a better flatmate."

"Yeah, she's lovely."

"Lovely," she quoted in an obtuse tone without a whiff of mockery. She went on: "What else do you think of her? It seemed as if you guys really hit it off. Do you think there might be something there?"

"What do you mean?" he replied defensively. He didn't like where this was going because he couldn't tell where it was going. Her words, transcribed, would have read like jealousy, but when she spoke them, they didn't sound like jealousy at all.

"You don't think she's beautiful?"

He didn't reply. If this wasn't a rhetorical question she would ask it again.

"I think she is. I think she's absolutely beautiful!"

He wasn't going to fall for any female dating traps. "Yes, I agree with you. But I'm not interested in her—sexually or romantically." He immediately regretted dichotomising his qualification and prayed she hadn't picked up on it. He said something, anything, to distract: "And I wouldn't go there. You know that. Or at least I hope you know that."

Not being able to read her face was making him uneasy. "Listen, what are you doing today? If you're not busy maybe we can meet up for a hot drink and a chat? We didn't get much of a chance to catch up at your birthday party."

"I know. I'm sorry. But there were so many people at the party that, if you think about it, I probably got on average no more than ten minutes of conversation with each one."

"Yeah, parties be like that sometimes."

"But we're catching up now!" she added cheekily with reconciliatory intent.

"Yes, but I much rather talk in person. I'm just not very good at this talking on the phone thing."

"What 'talking on the phone thing'? What are you some sort of time traveller from the Victorian era?"

"Funny," he said. "I think it's because I can't see the other person's face, so I can't tell if I'm being mis-understood, or ignored, or whatever."

"Well, granted, talking in person has its advantages, but so does talking on the phone. 'What advantages?' I hear you ask. Well, Miguel, that's a good question! Thank you for asking. You'll be pleased to find out that talking on the phone has, beyond all the obvious practical advantages, some advantages relevant to the early stages of courtship. 'An example?' Sure, I'll give you an example! A phone call lets you talk without the physical self-awareness that comes from being in front of someone you fancy, or without the pressure that your date might dive in for the kiss when you're least expecting it! Now, isn't that a reassuring thought?"

He laughed. He loosened up. He lay on his bed and

resumed his default position for talking on the phone with a girl. "That's an acute observation," he said in his huskier voice.

"Soon you'll discover that all of my observations are!"

"Ha!"

"Anyway, make yourself comfortable."

"I am."

"Good, because there are a few things we didn't talk about on our date or on my birthday that I think we should talk about now."

He tensed up a little again. "What's that?"

"Politics. And religion. And past—"

He burst into laughter.

She didn't.

"Oh, you were being serious?" He remembered how little she had given away on their first date. Maybe she was trying to compensate now. "So you really wanna talk about that stuff?"

"I do. I think it'll be a good way for us to get to know each other. And I also think it'll go a long way towards helping you get rid of your phone phobia."

"What?"

"You can thank me later."

"I don't have a phone phobia," he protested. "But don't they say never talk about politics and religion—"

"On the first date? Sure they do, but we already had that. Besides, Maria tells me you have some quite novel opinions on some rather contentious topics, and I'd like to hear them."

He was over the moon to hear that his feminism speech to Maria had worked—he knew it would—but he had to play it cool now lest he revealed his tricks.

"So tell me, what's your religion?"

"Don't have one."

"Hea-then," she said in a slow mutter as if she were jotting down the word. "And do you believe in an omnipotent, omnipresent, and benevolent God?"

"No."

"He-re-tic," she continued with her game.

"What are you doing?" He couldn't tell if she was really taking notes or just pretending.

A burst of laughter was her answer.

She was irresistibly adorable when she laughed so heartily. He felt her playful energy tingle through his body, from his sinus up to the soles of his feet.

It took her a while to finish laughing. "Oh my god, I'm bloody hilarious!"

"So then we're both areligious atheists? Thank god for that!"

"Ha! Good one!" she exclaimed in recognition of a linguistic construction so steeped in irony that it could only have been intentional. "But no, I wouldn't consider myself areligious nor atheistic. Once upon a time I might have, but these days, if I'm going to be labelled anything, I'd prefer to be labelled a secular humanist."

"I see," he said economically, too busy rehashing his previous sentence, not wanting the joke to go over his head but definitely not willing to have her explain it.

"Well, this isn't so hard. We could have done this on our first date!"

"But then again, one of us might have turned out to be a Scientologist or a Jehovah's Witness or something!"

"Ha! Yeah, that would've been... interesting," she said.

"And when you say 'interesting' what you really mean is

'awkward and the end of that conversation!'"

"No, I think it'd be kind of interesting to meet someone who's deep in a cult and to hear all their crazy stories."

"Actually, you're right. After watching The Book of Mormon, I—"

"Oh my god, I really wanna watch that!"

"Oh you should, it's hilarious."

"I know! Everyone keeps saying it."

"I will take you one day."

"I will love you until the end of time if you do."

They laughed. They sighed. They took a brief moment to think about how well the conversation was flowing.

He could get used to this. He initiated the second topic: "Okay. Politics!"

"Yes, Politics."

"Which ideology do you subscribe to?"

"Live and let live."

"Live and let live... I guess that makes you a liberal?"

"I would say I'm a staunch liberal on most points," she said. "Except in the governing of the commons, where I believe in strict central planning, and in trophy hunting, where I'm torn. What about you?"

"I think I'm quite liberally minded too. But then again, it's all relative, isn't it? And it varies. Maybe to you or somebody else, I'll sound conservative on some points."

"Well, let's find out. Let's run through some of the most prominent points."

"Alright, let's start alphabetically," he jested.

"Sounds like a plan."

"A. Let's see. Okay, I got a good one. Abortion!"

"Abortion?"

"Yes."

"I see we're diving straight into the deep end."

"We don't have to talk about it if you don't want," he said. "I'm sure there's something else beginning with A."

"No, no, let's. Let's talk about abortion." This was not a good topic for her, but she didn't want to give off that impression. "Tell you what. Why don't you tell me how you feel about it."

"Okay, well, I personally think that it's a woman's right to choose."

"However..."

"That being said, I also think that if I were a woman, which I'm not—"

"I know."

"But if I were, then there would be very few instances where I would choose to abort."

"How come? Are you feeling broody?"

"No, not at all! I don't think I have a single paternal bone in my body—except possibly my coccyx."

"Your coccyx?"

"Possibly."

"Is that the name you've given to your penis?"

"Haha! No, that's a legit bone."

"So that's the name of your erections?"

"Hahaha! No, no, no, that's the name of the last bone in the spine, the tailbone!"

"Oh! Hahaha! Damn, I completely misunderstood all that. Haha!"

"Told you it was easy to be misunderstood on the phone."

"Still, a small price to pay, I say. Anyway, so what would you do if some random woman you'd slept with called you today and told you she was pregnant by you?"

"Some random woman?"

"Some woman."

"Well, nothing. I could never, as a man, tell a woman what to do with her body."

"Yeah but isn't that the first thing they teach you men to say in Man School?"

"But it's the truth."

No reply.

"I mean, okay, I suppose it would depend on how well I knew her."

"How well you knew her?"

"In the sense that it might be easier to have an open and honest conversation with her if I knew her well."

"Okay," she said sceptically. "What kind of conversation?"

"About my feelings about the situation."

"So tell me what those are."

"Well, I guess it would all boil down to how long she's been pregnant for," he said. "Because I'm not at all comfortable with the idea of terminating a pregnancy past the embryonic period."

"Now you're speaking your mind. Continue."

"You know I recently saw a scan of a ten-week-old foetus, and it was fully formed with ten fingers and ten toes and all its milk teeth present—inside the jawbone obviously—but still, only ten weeks! That picture changed my entire outlook on abortion. I think I would find it very hard to support an abortion that late, and I think I would feel guilt and regret if I did."

"I see. So would you then try to convince her to keep it?"

"I wouldn't tell her what to do, but I guess I would ask

her to think about the baby, maybe remind her that it already has a beating heart and everything, maybe show her that scan that I saw. I don't know. What would you do?"

"I wouldn't consider aborting past the embryonic stage either, not unless the baby was diagnosed with an incurable disease that threatened its life or mine."

"Yes, I agree with you."

"Anyway, what's next on your alphabetical list of party icebreakers?"

"Ha! Well, let's see... I can't think of anything beginning with B," he said. "So should we skip to C and stay on this life-or-death topic and talk about capital punishment?"

"Capital punishment is fine by me."

"Oh, you're a proponent?" he jested.

"Hahaha! Nooo..." she sang in a deep pitch with vibrato. "Far from it!"

"Okay, so you're definitely against it."

"Yes," she said. "But don't get me wrong. I'm not one of those people who wholeheartedly believe that killing someone for their crimes is always morally wrong."

"Oh no?"

"Of course not!"

"You don't believe in salvation and all that?"

"Man, fuck that! Some sickos are way beyond salvation."

"Haha!"

"I mean, yes, in an ideal world punishment should be about rehabilitation, not just retribution and incapacitation. But then again, in an ideal world we wouldn't have crime in the first place, so..."

"You're funny."

"It's funny but it's true."

"So if you're not against capital punishment for moral reasons, then what are your reasons?"

"The thing is, capital punishment is a slippery slope fraught with grave repercussions."

He asked her to explain.

"Well, the first problem I have with it is that the arbitrary line in the sand which delineates the crimes that should be punishable by death is prone to human error and the vagaries of cultural norms. The second problem I have with it is that the judicial system has never been perfect. Sometimes guilty criminals get off scot-free, and sometimes innocent people get convicted. The risk that an innocent person could be wrongly killed by the state is, in itself, enough reason for me to oppose the death penalty."

"Those are two very legitimate concerns you raise. And what do you think about the death penalty as a crime deterrent?"

"That's what regular sentences are for—including the life sentence."

"Yes, I suppose so," he said. "Okay, we're getting through these pretty efficiently and without wanting to kill each other. This is rather remarkable!"

"I know, right! Okay, what should we talk about next? What starts with D...?"

"Er... drugs?"

"Yes, drugs. Good one! We can talk about drug policy next. Right, where do you stand on the spectrum between zero tolerance and total legalisation?" A part of her wanted him to be in favour of complete legalisation, while the other part wanted him to be dead set against it so she could test her persuading skills.

"I don't know. I don't think there's an easy solution to

the drug problem," he said, "but I do think the current policy is very hypocritical."

"How so?"

"Some banned drugs, like weed and hash, are not as bad for your health as the authorities will have you believe, and definitely safer than alcohol, which is totally legal. While some others, like crack and heroin, are extremely bad for your health, but not that much more dangerous than the opioids, benzos, and amphetamine derivatives that are also legal, albeit with a prescription."

"That is true."

"I think all substances—food and drugs—should be classified according to their health risks only. This government's Class-A/B/C taxonomy is complete bullshit, and it confuses the vulnerable people who don't have the capacity or the inclination to do proper research."

"I believe in complete legalisation," she said.

"Really?"

"Yeah."

"Like, all drugs?"

"Yes."

"All of them."

"Yes!"

"I don't know about that, Elsa."

"Why?"

"Because drugs like crack and heroin kill people and ruin lives."

"Yeah but so does sugar."

"You can't compare crack with—"

"Yes I can."

"Okay, let me put it this way. I would like the health authorities to send a clear and honest message to the population about what is harmless, what is harmful in large amounts, and what is pure poison and should be avoided at all cost."

"Fair enough, but I think your viewpoint is too idealistic, and I hope you won't mind me saying so."

"Not at all!" he said. "Please go ahead."

"Well, I think we have to be pragmatic and accept that there's a special type of person that will always want to get high. And to that person, the health risks of drugs, let alone their legal status, will never be a primary concern. So if we can't stop them from getting high—and I would argue, with history on my side, that we can't—then all that remains for us to do is to put together policies that minimise the total social costs of their highs."

"Hmm... Like what kind of policies?"

"Well," she said brimming with energy, "as a first step we need to decriminalise personal consumption of all drugs—just like they did in Portugal—to reassure users that they can seek help without fear of prosecution. In my opinion, the most important reason for decriminalisation is to shift the discourse of drug overuse from a criminal problem to a medical and social one."

"You know, that reminds me. When I visited Lisbon I saw a lot of heroin addicts casually chilling in an area that was literally swarming with police. It was like watching one of those nature documentaries where the wildebeests are tentatively drinking from the same waterhole as the nonchalant lions."

"Really?"

"Yeah, the juxtaposition was striking. It made for some thought-provoking photographs, but I couldn't figure out how to publish them without being exploitative, so in the end I just kept them in my private portfolio. But I digress," he said. "Please continue."

"No, no, that's really interesting..."

"First we need to decriminalise consumption, and then?"

"Right, and then we should go one step further and completely legalise the sale of all drugs. This would generate substantial tax revenue for the government; furthermore, it would allow for strict regulations so that consumers can get the unadulterated product—because often it's the substances that dealers use to cut the drugs that are the most harmful. No country has done this yet although some states in the US, most notably California, have completely legalised cannabis now."

"You really think that's the path we should pursue."

"Yes, I really do."

"You don't think that would just give rise to a whole generation of addicts?"

"I'm not worried about that. Most likely casual usage of mild drugs would increase, but that's not necessarily a bad thing. And the real victims of drug addiction would undoubtedly benefit because we would be able to track consumption and channel resources to those areas and individuals that are most at risk."

"Maybe..."

"Not maybe, definitely! Haha!"

"Ha! Well, okay, it might be worth giving it a try to see if it works," he said. "Even if only to end the War on Drugs that the US has been waging in Latin America with such catastrophic results."

"Yeah, that's a whole other reason."

They went quiet for a second. There was harmony in

their silence and an undercurrent of accomplishment.

"We're doing really well," she said.

"Yeah, I would say so. But let's not continue with the alphabet, please. I'm a too intimidated to discuss E with someone who's doing a PhD in Ecological Economics!"

"Ha! Fair enough. Anyway, I think we have a pretty good idea of where we stand on politics."

"Yes, it's been an interesting convo," he said, "but there's one more date taboo we haven't talked about yet."

"Ooh, I love taboos. What is it? Tell me!"

"Sex..." And he crossed his fingers in the hope that she might be a freak and this conversation might be about to get really interesting.

"Really?"

"Yeah, you still haven't told me what you're into."

"No, I mean, is sex really a taboo? Because Maria tells me that every guy she's ever met on Tinder has tried to bring up the topic of sex on the first date—some even before the first date."

"Yeah, I suppose you're right," he said in full retreat mode. "Times have changed."

"But you know what's apparently a super taboo? Past relationships! I read an article recently in a women's magazine that warned against talking about past relationships—as if it was literally the worst thing you could do. Can you believe it?"

"Oh, definitely. Nobody wants to listen to their date complain about their ex—or even worse, praise them!"

"I know, right? So, Miguel, tell me about your most recent relationship."

"What?"

"When did it start, how did it start, when did it end, and

why did it end?"

"Are you serious?"

"And don't lie to me..."

"I wouldn't lie, but my most recent relationship was almost a decade ago now."

"That's interesting in itself. Tell me more."

"You really wanna hear about it?"

"Yes, I do. But on one condition," she warned. "That you don't ask me to reciprocate."

But she didn't tell him why. She didn't tell him that it saddened her and riddled her with guilt. She didn't tell him how much of an accomplishment it had been for her to overcome the death of that relationship. She just told him that she didn't feel like talking about it.

Of course, her ominous request only served to spark his curiosity. Why didn't she feel like talking about her ex? And why would she ask him to talk about his past relationships if she wasn't willing to reciprocate? For a brief moment, he childishly considered refusing to share his story unless she shared hers, but he accurately assessed that he held no leverage, so he relegated himself to telling her his story. His only consolation: the thought that he would be able to lie just like she'd asked him not to, because they were talking over the phone like she'd forced him to. Notwithstanding his twisted consolation, Miguel went on to give Elsa the true version, unabridged. Why? Because he was subconsciously seeking her validation.

5 AMANDA

Miguel's first few months with Amanda—the period following his mother's death—were the numbest and haziest of his life. He had become trapped inside an intangible transparent film that prevented his environment from interacting with his senses. And whereas his father's death was marked by brutal floods in his head, suffocating pressure in his throat, and vicious cramps across his extremities, on this second heartbreak, the malevolent currents in his head had vaporised leaving only a light, gaseous space where his endless rumination would fester.

Furthermore, he was no longer one. There was him, and then there was his body—and the two were only weakly connected. He mostly resided inside of his body, somewhere in the back of his skull where he could watch the outside world through his body's eyes like two security monitors. From there he retained the power to suggest movement, speech, and thought, and for the most part, his body would oblige—at least on the first two counts. But occasionally he would be pulled outside of his body and be made to observe it in the third person. And then he would become a powerless spectator to his thoughts, words, and actions. These spells were terrifying and unpredictable, and as a result, he never quite felt safe in his body.

Amanda had watched over Miguel at rock bottom ten thousand meters in the sky, but his condition hadn't scared her; in fact, it was she who persuaded him to move in just ten days after they had met. Her idea made practical sense: she would be getting the perfect house sitter while she was away on work, and he would be saving money on rent while he figured out what to do next. However, the real reason for her suggestion had not been as pragmatic, nor benevolent.

Amanda was beautiful and polite. These two qualities had throughout her life provided her with an almost suspiciously large network of friends, colleagues, acquaintances, and of course suitors. But she'd never really cared for most of those countless faces that made her popular. Leon, her younger brother, was the only person she'd ever really cared for. He'd been born twelve years after her with a debilitating disability, and throughout his short life, she'd been his main carer in all but legal terms. Unfortunately, due to his deteriorating condition, Leon had recently passed away peacefully in his sleep.

Leon's death had left Amanda desolate, but she hid it very well from everyone around her because she felt no desire to share her feelings with anyone. That changed the day she met that lone broken stranger on her plane. Miguel kindled that desire, and she noticed it, but she promised herself that she wouldn't unburden herself to him because he was too vulnerable. Her twenty-nine years to his twenty-one reinforced that notion, as did his deteriorating mental health. (By the second week of his moving into her apartment, her prediction that he would slip into a depression would be confirmed. His pervasive guilt complex might have been nothing more than a quirky personality trait, but his unnaturally low sex drive, unsustainable lack of appetite, and irregular sleeping patterns would give it away.) Thus she maintained her facade of dependability, of solidity, of invulnerability, all—she told herself—in order to support him better. But her reticence wasn't all altruism; unbeknown to her, he was precisely what her ego craved. His misery gave form to her experience and function to her existence.

Amanda wasn't exactly sober when she met Miguel, but she hid it very well from everyone around her, including him. Her first fix, on the day of Leon's death, had come courtesy of his leftover painkillers and anticonvulsants. She stayed high for the following few days right up to the funeral. She liked the serenity the medicine restored in her and was astonished by how well she could function under its influence. It made her feel like her pre-death self, and this was of great comfort because she was afraid of losing herself. After the funeral, she took stock of the remaining medicine and began to ration it. For a while, she only used it to supplement her regular vodka sodas and THC vape oil on those nights when Leon's absence dawned unbearably heavy. But even so, she soon started running dangerously low.

Serendipitously, it was the day Amanda met Miguel that her addiction mutated into something more sinister. After giving him some sedatives on the plane, she realised how easy it would be for her to steal from the airline's in-flight medicine kit—all she would have to do was misreport the amount of medicine given to a panicky passenger. This was a good scheme, but it only lasted a few weeks because there simply weren't enough panicky passengers and because she wasn't able to report having dispensed more than a threshold amount per passenger without raising a red flag. Then one day, in an apparent stroke of genius, it occurred to her that she could safely procure more drugs by giving panicky passengers placebos and keeping the entire reported amount for herself. She was proud of her new plan, but she must have known on some level that this cunning was symptomatic of her growing addiction.

Unsurprisingly, Amanda was eventually found out. Her captain Antwan, a French veteran with several decades of flying experience, pulled her aside one day, told her that he knew, and suggested she request sick leave on the grounds of mental illness. 'Suggested' is a bit of a euphemism, but Antwan did offer to support her application and even recommended a good doctor who worked with the airline's medical insurance, a specialist who had helped him in the past. Thus she went home and told Miguel that she was taking some time off work due to Flight Fatigue—which, as she would have him believe, was a form of stress not uncommon among those in the airline industry.

They both welcomed her time off work. Amanda was now getting a constant supply of prescription drugs as well as a sabbatical of sorts at full salary, albeit at the cost of weekly sessions with the insurance policy shrink; and Miguel, who by then had developed an intense reliance on her for his emotional wellbeing, was now spending less time alone. But most importantly, their asymmetric co-dependency had remained intact, and he hadn't stopped looking up to her as a source of strength and support; on the contrary, she'd gradually taken on an even more maternal role, employing an improved communication style lifted straight out of her therapy sessions.

From the beginning of their relationship, Amanda had subconsciously feared the day when Miguel would no longer need her care. This was eventually made evident to her during a particularly draining therapy session. Sadly, following her realisation, she became obsessed with the thought that Miguel too would sooner or later leave her behind. And this inevitability consumed her, which is why she ashamedly obliged when he asked her one cruel night if he could try one of her benzos.

As the days and weeks passed, owing to his omnipresent fog of despair and to her mysterious omnipotence, Miguel began to harbour an unnerving distrust of her ostensible benevolence. And with all of their free time spent mostly at home, this new look in his eyes could hardly go unnoticed. Eager to fill the emptiness in his stare and anxious to feed her unquenchable addiction, Amanda began doling out more and more drugs, each pill a strategically timed depth charge parting through his fog and prompting a valiant attempt at recapturing his trust in her.

This reliance on self-medication to combat their ennui and conjure up positivity was never going to end well for either of them. Amanda's addiction had fully ensconced itself in her mind, out of sight but in control; meanwhile, Miguel's addiction was suffocating his depression prematurely—before he got a chance to confront it—and replacing it with something even more malignant. Of course, at their pace, they soon ran out of medicine. But Amanda, ever the provider, unhesitatingly went down the black-market route. And that's how they started experimenting with uppers: coke, a magical touch of confidence; speed, an ancestral curse of energy; ecstasy, a nuclear explosion of fantasies. Nothing lasts forever, and in the dregs of their hangovers, his distrust of her festered insidiously.

In an attempt to forge into their true form his mercurial

feelings towards Amanda, Miguel made it his mission to collect immutable evidence of her paranormal metamorphosis from an impostor beyond the transparent film to the infallible missionary of transcendental truths— and down again. He picked up an old film camera and began studying her body language at home through the rangefinder. The spiritual transparency he was looking for could only be teased out ritually, so rather than outsource the process, he learnt how to develop film and print photographs from a makeshift darkroom in their apartment. There he spent hours waiting for Amanda to emerge in a new light, but to his frustration, no new wisdom emanated from the photographic emulsion. Inauspiciously, all his pictures of her were shrouded by a mist of deception.[3]

With his curiosity insatiate, Miguel invested in an SLR camera body and a couple of lenses and started tailing Amanda on the rare occasions she left the apartment without him. The first few times he lost her before she reached her destination, and a few times after that he successfully followed her until her destination but discovered nothing of note: just her walking alone in the park or picking up from her dealer or something similarly benign. But far from suffering his new investigative role, he cherished it because from a young age he had frequently

---

[3] Gaze at a picture long enough and a nuanced story will begin to reveal itself: the projection of your preconceptions. Do this while high and you might take on a mystic level of sensitivity, igniting a light in your deepest recesses which shines through your most primal fears and casts immense their shadows.

fantasised about being a fly on the wall, and this assignment was piercing through his present condition and tapping into that juvenile excitement.

Then one day, Miguel followed Amanda for over an hour to an out-of-town storage park. Through a telephoto zoom lens he captured her fingers quiver as she unlocked the padlock, her body hesitate as she lifted the shutter door, and her gait stutter as she walked into the garage. He opened the aperture to capture a brighter image and saw her crying on her knees hunched over an empty wheelchair. He unconsciously lowered his camera and with a deep breath inhaled some of her pain. He unscrewed the lens hood, put on the lens cap, and headed home.

The moment he got back, he walked straight into his darkroom to develop the negatives. While he waited for the film to dry, he went on his computer to try to find some clues online as to who the wheelchair might have belonged to, but he didn't know where to begin. Then he considered combing the apartment for clues, but he gave up before even trying; after what he'd seen that day, he knew she wouldn't have kept any relevant belongings at home. Finally, he just poured himself a cold beer and swallowed a Special K and spread himself on the rug on the living room floor to listen to Kid A.

Once the album finished, around the same time as the ketamine was losing its grip, he took a magnifying glass to his negatives and saw the same vulnerability in Amanda that he'd witnessed as he'd shot the picture. And where another might have seen a broken woman, he finally saw Amanda whole. Then his mind's eye wandered back to that wheelchair he'd never heard about which had triggered those tears he'd never seen before. Suddenly he had the thought to google Amanda's surnames. He rushed back to his computer and quickly found the source of her tears: Leon Fernandes Carvalho, her younger brother. There was a Facebook page dedicated to his memory. He had loved animals. There were several pictures of Leon and Amanda in a farm feeding sheep and riding donkeys. There were even some pictures of them in a lagoon swimming with dolphins. And he'd been an avid Atlético de Madrid supporter. There was a picture of him with Diego Forlán, their latest superstar signing, in the middle of the Vicente Calderón pitch.

It is ironic but true that Miguel's uncovering of Amanda's secret marked the turning point at which his distrust of her started to disintegrate. This accelerated process was briefly accompanied by relief before being swiftly followed by guilt, guilt as it suddenly dawned on him that none of the feelings she'd asserted to have for him could rationally be thrown into doubt by her secrecy, whereas he'd shown himself to be untrusting and untrustworthy by doubting her and furtively following her. But then a figment of hope began to flicker inside him as he succumbed to the realisation that the time he'd spent photographing her was the first time since his mother's death that he'd felt a genuine sense of passion and excitement—while sober. The hope spread until it burned down every last lie, excuse, and rationalisation, leaving only the raw courage needed to accept the facts of his chemical and psychological dependency.

Miguel spent a couple of days grappling with his revelations before arriving at a conclusion, then waited another couple of days for Amanda to be relatively sober before sharing it with her. First, he confessed to having followed her and sincerely apologised for it. Second, he told her that he was an addict and wanted to quit. Third, he urged her to use this moment as an opportunity to reflect about her own state of mind, to acknowledge any emotion that she might be feeling, and to be honest with herself as well as him going forward. Amanda's energy roiled under her silence; her defence mechanism went into overdrive. By way of rationalisation, she focused solely on his betrayal of her trust. But he didn't try to defend his actions; he humbly deferred and reiterated his apology. And that's when she burst. Her persona of care and affection collapsed into a singularity then, in its inverse form, exploded outwards in every direction. Foul shards of hate lacerated his identity and severed his courage. Her fury left him no choice but to flee. She was left alone in a screaming chamber of memories. Endless visions of Leon spewed from within and wrenched at her heart. By the end of this torment, she had lost all sense of self. She couldn't define herself without her brother.

Miguel texted Amanda the morning after. She didn't reply. He waited. He texted and called her the following day. She still didn't reply or answer, so he immediately went to check up on her. When he entered her apartment—he still had the keys—he saw her passed out on the couch next to the coffee table where a lighter, a spoon, and a syringe lay. He'd never known her to take heroin before. She was unresponsive and he was scared. He called an ambulance and watched over her until it arrived then followed it to the hospital.

They didn't let him sleep in the hospital, so he went home. He couldn't sleep there either, and he came dangerously close to relapsing, but he managed to transmute his temptations into energy to pack all his belongings and completely move out before dawn. Incredible alchemy. In the morning, he headed straight to the hospital to speak to Amanda, to end their toxic relationship. But she spoke first. She told him she'd woken up from an epiphany in a lucid dream and spent the rest of the night thinking. She could see everything clearly now. She began by apologising for having used him and for not having been totally honest with him, but she swore that her feelings for him were one thing that had been one hundred per cent real. She continued by acknowledging she was an addict and by letting him know that she would be checking in to rehab, to this one place that her therapist had recommended. She concluded by telling him that their journey together had arrived at a juncture where it was bifurcating into individual paths that they would have to travel at their own pace, because the loss that connected them was holding them back, and they deserved an honest opportunity to heal from it.

As of today, Miguel and Amanda have both been clean for years. Shortly after their separation, Miguel moved back to London this time to pursue a career as a documentary photographer. Since then he has devoted his energy to showcase people fighting to overcome adversity, and he has gained a small but active following for it. And Amanda, after a few years battling her addiction in and out of rehab, eventually found solace—and victory—in a secluded permaculture community in the Portuguese countryside. She then moved to Holland with a friend from the community and together they opened a travel agency specialising in holidays for disabled persons of all ages. She dreams of building and running her own health resort one day. She has an idea for a sustainable retreat with an animal sanctuary, physical activities, and creative workshops—all designed to be sensory-friendly.

6 THE KISS
(PART 1: GALLERY & PHOTOGRAPHY)

Elsa spent the rest of her Sunday thinking about Miguel, about relationships, about her past...

She woke up on Monday inexplicably startled by his absence. She had felt his body, his warmth, his presence in those elusive moments before waking. This disintegration of her imagination's manufacture left a mould which was quickly filled with longing. But the mould was undefined, so her longing failed to set and instead cascaded back into the unremembered recesses of her subconscious.

While eating her usual weekday breakfast of raw oats and chia seeds soaked overnight in coconut milk, a thought struck her: she had no idea what he liked to eat for breakfast, or if he even ate breakfast at all. This put into perspective how little she knew about him. Suspicion took over. She didn't want to make the mistake Amanda had made, so she told herself she would only act on her feelings once she felt sure that what had attracted her to him after hearing his story was his honesty and his strength—not her sympathy. Two days later, partly satisfied with her emotional vetting process and partly just tired of self-constraint, she invited him to a photography exhibition on Friday.

They had scheduled to meet outside Goodge Street station at 11am. She arrived first, but she didn't know it yet. She looked around and couldn't see him, so she thought she would call him to let him know that she was there, just in case he was somewhere nearby killing time. But when she took her phone out of her pocket and saw 10:52am on the lock screen, she decided not to because she didn't want to seem too eager. So she went on Instagram to pass away the eight minutes remaining until eleven. She went straight to her favourite profile, a curation of hyper-cute animal memes that never ceased to amuse her. Its latest post: an elephant charging into a shallow but fast-moving almost white-water river to save a man who looked like he was drowning. She knew the video could easily have been staged, but she didn't much care because elephants were still cute as fuck in her eyes. In fact, she had a long-running conviction that the Kinder mascot should have been an elephant, not a bloody hippopotamus. "Nothing against hippos," she thought, "since they're not to blame for how Mother Nature made them, but a hippo would never save a human from drowning. A hippo in a river is no less dangerous than a crocodile! Maybe that's what they should have chosen for their mascot: a crocodile. Kinder Kroc! With a K for visual as well as phonetic alliteration. And for legal reasons, since it's easier to defend Kroc from copyright infringement than Croc." She raised her head from her phone and looked around. Nothing. She moved on to a video of a very happy slow loris with its arms over its head. Its caption: "I'm only as venomous as you are allergic!"

"How cute," he announced abruptly within whispering distance to her ear.

She jumped. "Fuck! You scared me. What are you some sort of ninja? Don't ever sneak up on me like that again!"

He laughed so hard at her reaction. "I would've never guessed you'd jump like a little kitten!"

"Asshole! I'll get you back for this sooner or later." And she jokingly pursed her eyes into a menacing squint. "Anyway, how good of you to finally make it!" She put her phone in her belt bag and leaned in for a hug.

"Don't try it, I'm right on time," he said mid-hug. "And I look forward to your doomed revenge attempt," he added as they disengaged.

On their way to the Alison Jacques Gallery—a five-minute walk to Berners Street—they summarised their work week. He spoke about a military hospital he'd visited as part of his research for a piece on veterans' health. She spoke about a computer model she'd contributed to as part of a petition calling for a plastic tax.

"Thanks again for this. I'd actually heard about it and was meaning to check it out."

"You're welcome. Are you a fan of Mapplethorpe? Have you ever seen his work before?"

"Yeah, I think I've seen most of it."

"Oh," she said somewhat disappointed.

"No, it's fine. I mean, the guy's like a legend in the world of photography, so of course I've looked into him before. Also, he's been dead for decades, so it's not like he's constantly releasing new stuff."

"Ah, okay. And are you a fan of his? You didn't answer."

"I wouldn't say I'm a fan. So the guy can be shocking to the point of offensive at times. But I like that. That's part of what made him so revolutionary at the time. And even to this day, his imagery is still considered profound despite all the social progress that's taken place since his time."

"But..."

"However, his work is grossly overrated by self-regarding art critics who've never actually shot a worthwhile picture in their entire fraudulent lives."

"Oh, I didn't know this."

"Not many people do. But for example, his dominant and dangerous depiction of the black male body—a hyper-sexualised colonial fantasy of a race that he further subjugated through his indisputable mastery of light as well as through his celebrity status—while regarded as groundbreaking by some photography dilettantes, pales in comparison to the representations of, say, Lyle Ashton Harris or Malik Sidibe or Rotimi Fani-Kayode with regards to the issues of race, culture, and sexuality. But of course, they never got anywhere near as much mainstream recognition. And even though we can't know for sure whether that's because they weren't white, we do know for sure that they weren't white."

"Okay," she said with that inflexion that people sometimes use when they're impressed, the one that usually coincides with raised eyebrows and a recessed chin, the one that might be followed with them jokingly flicking the dirt off their shoulder with a single pinch of their shirt.

"Yeah, my bad. I often ramble on when talking about photography."

"No, no! I like it that you're this passionate about your work. It's very... positive." She didn't want to say 'attractive' and give him a big head.

"Anyway, so what made you want to see this exhibit?"

"Er..." And now she didn't want to lie, but she didn't want to come across as a philistine either.

He sensed her reluctance to answer. "Well?"

More silence.

"Wait, you don't actually know who Mapplethorpe is, do you? So how did you even come across this?"

"I know who he is!" she asserted before muttering: "(I googled him on my way here.)"

"And?"

"Well, you know..."

"I know what?"

"Look, the London Underground sucks, okay? There's no reception down there except in the platforms, so the Wikipedia article didn't load on time!"

"Haha! That's good, that's good," he said. "Now I'm really looking forward to this."

"Why?"

"You'll see."

And she saw as soon as they entered. Large-format black-and-white prints of what seemed like nothing but semi-erect penises, retro vaginas, and bare anuses. She was shocked on the inside but managed to retain her external composure. She struggled to appreciate the artistic and political merit of the work outside of its historical context. By today's digital standards, his studio pictures weren't all that remarkable; and as a social commentary, they were outdated (fisting might have been a big taboo back in the '70s, but these days it has its own Pornhub category).

Near the end of the small gallery, Elsa saw a picture which succeeded in cracking her deceptively cool demeanour: a naked man lying on his back hugging his knees to his chest presenting his genitals to the camera. Miguel took a few steps closer to her and asked for her thoughts. "His butthole is pouting," she said. This triggered a blast of laughter which spurred her on. "No, but seriously, look at it. It looks like it's blowing bubbles at the camera! Wait, do you reckon this was captured mid-fart?" Hearty bouts of laughter erupted deep from within his chest. "You know, if you squint, it kind of looks like a walnut." That was it. That sent him irreversibly into a fit. He couldn't stop now. He was bent over, holding his middle, gasping for air. Tears were running down his nose and dripping off its tip. The raucous was too much for this small gallery and its genteel visitors. She felt their heavy eyes. "Let's get out of here," she whispered to him. She put an arm around him and escorted him towards the exit.

He had to battle his spasming diaphragm to regain access to his vocal facilities. "Yeah, I think I've seen enough penises for one day," he managed to slip in during a trough of his laughter.

"I think I've seen enough penises for one month!" she replied as she leaned into him with an affectionate shoulder budge and dropped him a cheeky sucks-to-be-you wink that he missed because he was still struggling with his diaphragm. "Miguel, if you can hear me, come back to me."

"Hold on. Wait. Let me catch my breath..." And one huge sigh later: "Alright, alright. I think I'm back. Okay. Damn. Wow, that was intense... Right, let's see, er, what do you want to do now?"

She seemed to deliberate at first. Then she turned to face him, moved closer, and whispered sultrily in her best albeit still atrocious Italian accent: "Gamberetti e Spinaci linguini in Vapiano."

"Wow, I don't even know what you just said, but in that Nordic accent of yours it definitely makes me want to eat it."

"What nonsense! I said it in an Italian accent."

"Italian? Haha! What? Oh... Gamberetti e Spinaci," he repeated but in a perfect Italian accent. "As in, prawn and spinach."

She rolled her eyes.

"And there I thought you were talking about a Finnish dish or something."

"Whatever. You creamed your pants when I said it."

"Well, my pants are creamed alright. I'm just not entirely sure at which point I creamed them. Was it your impeccable Italian accent, or was it Mapplethorpe's wonderful walnut picture? Haha!"

"Hahaha! Well, that prawn and spinach dish is also full of cream. And I'm not joking when I tell you that I've often dreamed about burying my face in it." She let out a soft moan and with closed eyes licked her lips like LL. "Imagine being smothered by all that cream..."

"Let's go right now!" he said with a sense of urgency usually reserved for medical emergencies.

"Oh, now you want some too, huh? Trust me daddy—you're gonna love it."

A few seconds later, with his perilous sex-drive spike fast receding, he came back to his senses. "I'm not gonna lie. I'm curious and tempted. But I doubt I'll order any food because I'm actually really full. I had a massive English breakfast probably no more than an hour ago."

"Ah, what? That's no fun," she said stopping in her tracks.

"It'll be fine."

"No, it won't. Why do you have to be such a boner kill?"

"I'm happy to keep you company while you eat."

"No, let's not go then. I refuse to pig out in front of you all on my own."

"Why?"

"What girl do you know would want her date to sit there watching her scoff down a bowl (or two) of spaghetti?"

"Oh, c'mon, it's not that big a deal."

"Man, have you seen Beauty and the Beast? Well, I eat like the Beast in the scene when he's having dinner with Bella for the first time. Ooh, I have a great idea: let's go to the zoo!"

"Alright, yeah we can do that. But you're going to get hungry. I think you should have some pasta if you really feel like it."

"No, it's okay. I'll just get a Breakfast Club from Joe & The Juice and eat it on the way. And maybe also a bag of Sweet & Salt Popcorn from Pret."

"Damn! You've got it all figured out, don't you?"

After stocking up on her food, they took the Tube from Oxford Circus to Regent's Park. Sitting opposite them were a man and woman who were coming back from a family law office near the Strand where they had finally signed their divorce settlement agreement. There was a palpable serene lightness to their newborn resonant energies, and both Elsa and Miguel soon became enchanted by the ex-couple, staring at them in admiration, interpreting their closure as true love.

7 THE KISS
(PART 2: REGENT'S PARK & FOOD CHOICES)

They crossed the gates of Regent's Park in silence. Not so much the quietude bestowed by its greenery, but rather the interlude between the time an emotion gets felt and a thought constructed. An excitement akin to that experienced just before the start of a great journey ensconced in a familiarity usually reserved for the friends one grows up with. Potential, parity, unity... And there it was right in front of them: love, a monumental new truth! This edifice was ancient to her and alien to him, but the shadow it cast on them today was positively tranquil.

"You're going to make one lucky lady a very happy wife one day. You know that?" She wasn't one to play coy, but neither was she one to speak before she thought, so this off-the-cuff remark caught her a little off-guard.

It caught him a little off-guard too. "What made you say that?"

"Well, you know," she began with incandescent cheeks. "You're really nice to talk to, and you're not so bad to look at either!"

"Hmm..."

"You don't like taking compliments?" She tried to extinguish her embarrassment by owning up to her words, even if they seemed to have been uttered on her behalf by an autonomous agent.

"As it happens I don't, no. But that's not what I meant."

He'd been after the cause not a clarification of her comment. But maybe she didn't want to share what had prompted her thoughts, or maybe he'd been too ambiguous with his wording. So he tried again, with a leading question this time: "What did you make of that couple on the train?"

Eager to move the conversation along, she answered: "Oh-em-gee, they were sooo cute! I wanted to miniaturise them and put them in my pocket and carry them around with me all day and every few hours feed them Ferrero Rochers."

"Hahaha! Ferrero Rochers?" She was too fucking adorable, and he was getting hot with exasperation.

"Yes!"

He desperately needed to release his pent-up affection, but he successfully reigned it in. "But relative to the couple, wouldn't the Ferreros be huge? Like beachball size."

"What are you saying?"

"I'm just saying that giving someone half their body weight in refined sugar would probably kill them from an insulin spike or something. Remember what you said about sugar being comparable to crack?"

"What nonsense! You're being totally ridiculous. Why would I feed them real-size Ferreros? Obviously, I would shoot the Ferreros with the same shrink gun that I used to miniaturise the couple so that they'd be perfectly in proportion!"

Miguel let out the most raucous torrent of laughter that would be heard that day in any of London's Royal Parks. At this point, he just wanted to grab her by the shoulders, squeeze her towards him, and show her how happy he felt around her.

"On second thought, I might set the shrink gun strength to twenty-five per cent for the Ferreros and serve them fewer so that I can save some monies. Because lord knows Ferreros ain't cheap!"

"You're hilarious!"

"Ooh, let's take some selfies with these sculptures!"[4]

Par the course for a photographer, he didn't like having his picture taken (one of those off-putting clichés of life), but he suspected that he wouldn't have much say in the matter, so he didn't even try to refuse. Be water, my friend.

"If I had known we were going to Regent's Park, I would have brought my selfie drone." It was impossible to tell if she was joking or not. The tone was too goddamn neutral.

"It's such a beautiful day." Ah, that tried-and-tested weather deflection! But this time it was genuine. And Miguel just wanted to take a moment to acknowledge how good the weather was.

And it really was a beautiful day: crisp, sunny, and much warmer than the historical average for this time of year. But surprisingly, given that it was the middle of a weekday in autumn, the park was filled with people of all ages. Miguel offered half term as a possible explanation, so Elsa checked online for school holidays, but half term wasn't for another week or two (depending on the school).

They continued leisurely, taking in everything in their surroundings and nothing beyond it. They walked

---

[4] That summer Regent's Park became home to the inaugural Frieze Sculpture outdoor display, which was drawing to a close that weekend.

wordlessly shoulder-to-shoulder in tandem. She looked out to the vegetation around her and searched for any side effects of this preternatural October heat wave. He looked down at the gravel directly in front of him and watched the tip of his shoes alternately come in and out of his field of vision. A popcorn entered his frame unannounced, dancing in an unpredictable staccato. It died unavoidably, crushed under one of his marching feet. This unfortunate yet inconsequential casualty prompted him to redirect his visual attention back to Elsa. He followed her hand as it made the journey from inside the foil bag to the opening of her mouth, a journey so perfected that it made him wonder whether it might have been somebody else's popcorn that had fallen in front of him a few steps earlier.

"So how come you're a vegan then?" he asked her.

"What makes you say I'm a vegan?"

"Oh... Well, I'm pretty sure Maria mentioned it at your party."

"You mean at the party where we ate a strawberry gateau filled with layer upon layer of fresh cream?"

"That's so strange. I really thought Maria had said you were—"

"Maybe she did, maybe she didn't. Either way, at least one of you doesn't know what being vegan entails."

"Ouch! What do you mean? I know what being vegan entails."

"Really? Because I also distinctly remember telling you not even an hour ago that I wanted to eat creamy prawn and spinach linguini? So what kind of vegan does that make me then, a part-time one?"

"Oh yeah, you did say that. I don't know. I guess I wasn't thinking... Okay, so you're not a vegan then."

"No. Although in your and Maria's defence I did use to be vegan once, a long time ago in a galaxy far, far away."

"Aha! So you were a vegan at some point. I knew it! Okay, so what made you become a vegan and why did you stop?"

"What do you think are the reasons why someone might want to become a vegan?" She didn't mean to come across as patronising. She was just trying to be pedagogic in the best way she knew how: through participation.

"Er, I don't know... Health? Environment? Love of animals?"

"There you go."

"All of the above?"

"Yep."

"Alright. So why did you stop?"

"Well, I haven't stopped caring about animal welfare or my health. And I maintain that our industrial farming and fishing methods are a leading cause of environmental degradation. What's more, I never decided to stop being a vegan, because I never really identified as one. Yes, people called me that and I never corrected them. But all along I simply considered myself a plant-based eater who, by the way, would've killed and eaten just about any animal if my survival had truly depended on it—including humans. And today I'm still overwhelmingly the same: a plant-based eater. It's just that now I've broadened my food selection criteria to include social cohesion and raised the weight on the price and taste variables. Also, I've made all the weights dynamic so that variables are prioritised and deprioritised according to—" she looked at him in a belated act of self-awareness "—according to context." She allowed some time for him to digest her esoteric answer. After a brief moment of silence which was too long for her liking, she pithily summarised her position as if in admittance of some wrongdoing: "I was perhaps being too rigid and so I decided to loosen up a little."

"I see." And a neural pathway was spontaneously formed linking his understanding of her answer to his recollection of Siddhartha Gautama's Middle Way: happiness cannot be found in asceticism nor sybaritism.

"Basically I finally got the bug out my ass, much to everyone's delight!" Her jovial words, a clear internalisation of other people's opinions, carried with them a repressed hint of shame.

Miguel caught a whiff of it. "I wouldn't worry too much about other peoples' delight. At the very least because some people are sadists who find delight in the cruellest of things."

But she didn't want to come across as ungrateful for the honest feedback from her friends and family and therapists. So, in an expansive tone, she expounded on her self-acceptance: "I guess with time I have come to the realisation that life is for living. No one should deprive themselves of a chance to live fully, because neither a life of abstinence nor a martyr's death will redeem our sins."

"Rolling in the muck is not the best way of getting clean," he replied almost automatically while he dealt with the sudden obscurity shrouding her words. He sensed both melancholy and peace in equal doses but was unable to bisect her mood. He tried to make a light joke so as not to have the conversation be downcast. Sporting a devilish smile, he asked her: "Anyway, what do you know about sinning?"

"More than I care to share," she replied solemnly.

With his banter ineffectual, and unable to pursue her ominous answer without ignoring its content, he found himself deliberating over what to say next. In the end, he settled on returning to the topic of veganism. "Alright, so what do you call yourself if not a vegan?"

"Elsa—that's all I ever call myself." She paused to assess how that might have come across: defensive, borderline confrontational. This had not been her intention, so she went about explaining herself more generously: "I think labels, even in something as benign as dietary habits, can be unproductive if not counterproductive. The security and validation that we get from being part of an established group comes at the expense of thought independence and deprives us of the learning experience that comes from having to gain and defend our individuality." She was mostly satisfied with her elaboration, but she still felt the desire to compromise further and provide a direct answer to his question. "But to answer your most likely well-intentioned question, I suppose 'conscious omnivore' would be an apt name for the way I relate to food."

He gazed intently at her, ineluctably palpating the multidimensional shape of her essence. "You know, I really admire the way you think and express yourself... And yes, my question was most definitely well-intentioned!"

"Oh, so you can't take compliments, but you can dish them? What a lousy hypocrite!"

"Haha! No, but seriously, I don't know if you realise, but you have an incredible mind."

"I guess I am one of a kind." And she blew hot breath on her nails.

"How did you become..." And he saw her buff them against her top. "Wait." And he finally laughed.

"To answer your unfinished question: nobody can explain how I became this shining beacon of human progress. It's one of those great unsolved mysteries of science." His laughter began to snowball until it turned into an avalanche which knocked the wind out of him and left him bent over trying to catch his breath. "I think your humour might be suffering from premature ejaculation!" She looked around for witnesses in the same way that a dog owner might look around when he's thinking of not collecting a turd that his best friend just planted. "Come on, get up. It was only a little joke. No need to make a meal out of it."

But he couldn't stop laughing. And he couldn't speak. His voice had been annexed by his laughter. So he held up an arm to show her his palm. "Hold on. Stop. Give me a chance to catch my breath," is what this gesture meant.

Eventually, his laughter attack abated and Elsa, fearful of a relapse, seized the opportunity to resume walking. "What about you? What's your relationship with food like?"

"Well... I know you're not going to approve, but I really don't think about it at all. I just eat whatever's closest to me. Hugh Hefner probably had a more mindful relationship with his least favourite playmate than I do with my food."

"Haha! Well, who knows, maybe some of my good dietary habits will rub off on you. I'll start by teaching you a few easy recipes, like my world-famous lentil broth and my favourite salads."

"Seriously, I would love that. And I need that because currently it seems like I only eat junk food and only at irregular times. '5 A Day'? I'll be lucky if I get to five a week!"

"Hahaha! That's terrible. You should be more careful with what you eat now, or it might catch up with you later on in life."

"I know, I know, I know I have to change. I mean, I've seen the documentaries—Fast Food Nation, Forks Over Knives, What the Health, etcetera—and the evidence is compelling. But I'm still waiting for the day that I make a single conscious food choice."

"Maybe it just comes down to a lack of self-love."

"She tends to get deep with this food topic," he thought to himself. "But what is she trying to get at? Is she hinting that I may be self-sabotaging? Do I come across as having masochistic tendencies?" Wishing to conceal his inner monologue, he rushed to compose a disarming quip: "I'll try to nourish my inner child better from now on." But he missed his chance to vocalise it because she spoke before he did.

"Or maybe too much of it!" she jested.

He let out a quick laugh to be polite and to distract from the fact that he was now busy scrambling theories in his head about her true character. "Is she projecting? Is she secretly or unwittingly describing herself?"

"Or maybe you love yourself just the right amount, an amount commensurate with your spiritual worth, and the reason why you end up making food choices that you wouldn't make in forethought or retrospect is simply a very human mixture of present bias and optimism bias." She forwent one step, and then a second, and by the third she was asking herself why she'd stopped. She couldn't think of a why, but it had been a sort of motion sickness caused by her rapid change of direction from intellectualism to buffoonery and back. She squared up to him and said:

"Listen, you want shallow? Go date someone else." Then stood her ground, facing him defiantly, with no more than 30cm separating the tip of their noses.

Ultimatums, by design, demand an immediate response; their urgency is constructed to bring about a prompt resolution. Elsa was physiologically primed for whatever was to come next; Miguel was paralysed, transfixed by her eyes. Both their hearts were pumping adrenaline-filled blood. Perhaps the distance had closed to 25cm by now, but neither of them had noticed it; they were both engrossed in trying to understand this tense moment. She kept her eyes on his and waited for a reaction, unconsciously drawing closer to him. At 20cm he became aware of the creeping proximity and instantly got hard. She noticed the change in his eyes: intent. Freed from his initial paralysis, he was now singularly focused on kissing her lips. He grew optimistic. The setting, a sunny Regent's Park, was picturesque enough for the occasion. 15cm. He raised his right hand and covered the concave curve where her jaw met her neck. 10cm. She grew anxious. The setting, the middle of a field, was too exposed for the occasion. She raised her right hand and placed a cluster of popcorn almost on his lips. His eyes were burning with intent.

He shook his head. "You know that's not what I want right now."

"Your loss!" She killed the popcorn and licked the sugar and salt off her lips then fingertips. 20cm, 25cm, 30cm...

"You are truly unique. You know that?" And he artfully retraced his right hand in the most subtle and likely-to-save-face way possible. Smooth.

"Oh please, you're the bohemian snowflake!" And in

two plyometric skips, she was at a green metal bin three meters away discarding four grams of non-recyclable packaging.[5] She returned to him in the same haste. She slapped and rubbed her hands, took out a travel-size glycerine-based hand sanitiser from her eco leather belt bag, and used it as per the instructions which she had once read and still remembered. He was surprised by the proficiency with which she cleansed her hands. Her movements were perfectly coordinated, creating the illusion of choreography. "May I?" she asked as she put her arm in his with confidence and speed, not giving him time to nod until after the fact. "Thanks," she said. Then she leaned in on her tiptoes and kissed him on the cheek.

---

[5] Disappointingly, all metallised plastic film bags (so-called foil bags) used to package crisps and similar foodstuffs are currently non-recyclable.

8 THE KISS
(PART 3: ZOO & ECOLOGY)

Elsa and Miguel reached the zoo's entrance as a primary school class was on its way out. The children were expectably excited, and their chaperones a mixture of tired and alert. All the children had their faces painted and were dressed in animal costumes: black-and-white pandas, brown-and-yellow giraffes, orange-and-black tigers. Few things in life are as heart-meltingly adorable as kids in onesies.

"You see? This is why the zoo is a necessary evil," she said. "Look at these kids. Each one of them is potentially a future environmental champion."

"Evil? You mean keeping animals in captivity?"

She nodded.

"You know, I used to roll my eyes at those animal rights warriors who'd break out in hives at the mere sight of a zoo. But then I watched the documentary Blackfish, and now I really have to agree that some animals should never be kept in captivity."

"Well, in an ideal world, no animal would be forced to live in captivity. But the moral grounds for keeping an animal in a zoo vary depending on how we obtain the animal. Rescuing an animal from an inevitable human-caused death is not the same as stripping it from its natural habitat. And of course, how we maintain the animal is just as important, if not more. Clearly migratory or predatory animals will never be wholly fulfilled in captivity given that some of their instincts will be repressed. So I absolutely agree with you that keeping orcas in a small pool and forcing them to do tricks for food is inhumane."

"In-animal-ane?"

"Ha! Good one."

"Thanks. I just made it up. Haha!"

"I like it! I might start using it."

"By all means. It's open source."

"Perfect! But to continue. No zoo should ever be a fucking circus. And hopefully one day our social consciousness will evolve to a point where we don't need zoos, aquariums, and similar attractions. But until that day comes, we should keep them because they raise awareness. In fact, often they constitute the only point of contact with wildlife for large swathes of urban populations."

"Hence the 'necessary'?"

"Yes. In my opinion, it's the lesser of two evils."

Elsa and Miguel reached the counter where they were asked if it was just the two of them. It was. But Elsa had a voucher, somewhere in her belt bag, if she could just find it. She rummaged for a little longer and... and there it was! She paid for one adult ticket, and both of them walked through the gates.

"Oh and, Elsa, when you say that no animal should be forced to live in captivity. Do you then believe that all animals deserve to live free?"

"Of course!"

"What about pets, work animals, and livestock?"

"In principle, I don't have a problem with hunting animals or growing them for food. At the end of the day, we are biologically an omnivorous species, and by definition, omnivores eat other animals. And let's be reasonable, we're not even the only animal to farm other animals. For example, certain species of ants farm aphids for honeydew."

He nodded in assent.

"As for keeping animals captive for labour and company: I have no problem with it as long as the living conditions of the animal are such that it would freely choose to stay with its master if given the option of leaving."

He nodded again.

"That being said, I do of course have a problem with how a lot of these animals are treated in practice."

He gave his reply: "Your views are very reasonable. I think that with animal welfare, as with many of life's big questions, there's probably no definitive answer, but ultimately that's what makes these topics so exciting to explore intellectually..."

Elsa saw a face-painting stand. "Hey, look! We can get our faces painted over there."

"And we can keep our faces unpainted everywhere else."

"Oh come on, it'll be fun."

"Fun?"

"Yes, so we can take selfies looking like animals!"

He chose not to dignify that with a response, but his expression spoke volumes.

"Please!"

"No."

"Please."

"No."

"Please."

"Why don't you just use a Snapchat lens?"

"A Snapchat lens? A Snapchat lens?!" This suggestion somehow got her fuming. "Listen, Miguel, you're going to come with me to get my face painted, and you're going to get yours painted too—and that's final."

"I'll go with you, but there's literally no way I'm getting my face painted," he said.

Ten minutes later...

"So, panda then?" checked the painter.

"Yes, Panda," confirmed Elsa.

And Miguel simply nodded in acquiescence.

"Alright, panda it is. And I usually say this to boys more than men but... please try to sit as still as you can, sir."

The three of them remained silent during the face painting. Miguel, with his eyes shut, in a meditative state; the painter, with her eyes fixed on his face, in a state of pure concentration; and Elsa, with a blank stare, distantly pensive.

She was replaying parts of their previous conversation about animal welfare, and one of his comments particularly stood out: "Your views are very reasonable." Such stark contrast from the feedback she received when she decided to embark on her PhD. It came from many places: from her friends, from her father, from the arcane rulings of research funding committees... "The topic is too radical," they said, "too extreme." Each time she wondered why they intoned that as if it were a bad thing. It always prompted her to think of great historical figures that had sat right in the middle of the spectrum of opinions, right on the fence of a conflict. Of course, she could never think of any. Controversy and Social Impact; once again she drew a Venn diagram in her mind with the latter enclosed within the former.

"So, Miguel," she said. "Who do you think are the radical thinkers in our society?"

He looked at Elsa for more.

"With regards to animal rights..."

He looked at the painter for permission to reply. He got it via a single nod after a few finishing touches.

"Well, you have radical thinkers on both sides of the aisle, right? There are those who don't give a flying fuck about animals, for who 'animal rights' is nothing more than an oxymoron; and there are those who maybe care a little bit too much about animals, for who an idea, or rather an ideal, becomes their prerogative."

"I think you're drawing a false equivalence between the two extremes."

The painter—an ambitious second-year zoology student who had taught herself how to face-paint as a backdoor into the institution that runs the zoo—liked where this discussion was heading and wished she got to face-paint adults more often.

"They're both entitled to their opinion, and they both have a right to voice it," Miguel said.

"Yes, but one side is trying to make the world a better place while the other is just trying to stop them."

"True. But unfortunately, to pass laws in a democracy, huge compromises have to be made to placate both sides— but most of all, to convince the majority in the middle."

"Ah, the majority," she said. "The apathy is strong among the majority."

"That's why the message has to be positive and motivational. And that's where environmentalists have, in my view, been failing: in driving a positive message that the average person wants to get behind. Although it's not entirely their fault. When trying to make the world a better place, you inevitably have to focus on the things that are wrong with it, because 'All is well' isn't exactly a soul-stirring call to arms! And I think that's why most environmentalists come across as a bit overly pessimistic, and why they don't make for the most sought-after guests at dinner parties. Haha!"

"Yes, unfortunately we do fall victim to people's tendency to shoot the messenger."

"So you've experienced it yourself in your line of work?"

"Oh, absolutely! Many people have resorted to personal attacks when they didn't like what I was saying."

"Really? What sort of personal attacks?"

"Nothing major, just the usual discrediting tactics."

"Like what? Give me an example."

"Oh, I don't know."

The painter surprised them both by giving an example: "I was called a hypocrite by some troll for taking part in Earth Hour."

"Earth Hour?" asked Miguel.

"Really?" Elsa had a good idea of where this was going, but she was keen to give the young girl a chance to tell her story.

"It's because during Earth Hour," began the zoology student and part-time face painter, "the drop in greenhouse gases has not been as big as some people thought, you know? And there have even been increases in some countries. It's all to do with, like, the efficiency of the light bulbs used and the cleanliness of the electricity flowing through the national grid at the time and stuff. It's all because it's night time during Earth Hour—well obviously not everywhere but, like, for the majority of the world's population anyways—so most people taking part will light up a few candles at home. But burning candles releases CO_2 because, well, because all combustion does really."

Elsa chose not to add that nearly all candles are made out of paraffin wax—a petroleum derivative with a high carbon content—because she didn't want to interrupt the young girl's flow.

"So let me get this straight," replied Miguel. "You're basically saying that during Earth Hour, if enough people switch from, say, LED bulbs powered by renewables to candles then world CO_2 emissions can actually increase?"

In some cities, there have been recorded increases in CO_2 emissions during Earth Hour from the hour immediately preceding it; however, none statistically significant when you control for the circadian rise in central heating at that time of night. But again, Elsa kept this to herself.

"Yeah," said the zoology student. "But the point I was trying to make, in vain, to this stupid cyber troll is that Earth Hour is not about reducing emissions for sixty minutes— it's all about, like, increasing awareness and reshaping our relationship with our planet and stuff."

"Right," said Miguel. "And if I've understood correctly then Earth Hour might still be beneficial in terms of emissions if we measure its effect over an entire year or something?"

"Exactly!" said the painter. "Although I don't know how we could ever empirically prove that, you know?"

"This is very interesting," he said. "I'm gonna look more into at home."

Elsa liked his inquisitive nature but warned him against expecting any definitive answers, especially online.

Miguel assured her that he was yet to find a definitive answer to any question worth asking.

Elsa repeated that line in her head. "I'm yet to find a definitive answer to any question worth asking." It was damn near prophetic. She asked him where he'd gotten it from.

He turned his palms and shrugged. "Nowhere. I just said it." Believe it or not, despite all their conversations so far, Miguel hadn't yet realised that Elsa was a hardcore sapiosexual, but the compositional and chromatic changes in her face now made him suspect it for the first time.

The painter also noticed Elsa's face morphing from the roaring tigress that she was thinking of painting to a purring kitten. "Us girls gotta stick together," she thought. So she tried to cut the tension: "Shall we get started on your face now?"

"Yes—actually, wait. Let me first get a picture of Miguel looking all cute and panda."

"Can we at least save the pictures for when we're both painted?" And Miguel got up from the stool.

"Okay, fine." And Elsa sat down on it.

"And what will it be for you?" the painter asked.

"I was thinking maybe a tigress."

"I was thinking that too—initially. But now that I'm looking at your face more closely, I think a butterfly would work better."

"Alright, I trust your judgement. Give me the most beautiful butterfly wings that ever flapped!"

"I'll try."

"I'm gonna go get something to drink. You guys want

anything?"

"Hmm... Yes, sparkling water, please."

"And you?"

"No, thank you," said the painter. "That's very kind of you though."

Before walking off, he threw one last glance at Elsa with his big panda eyes.

While Miguel was gone, the painter tried to have a girlie chat with Elsa about him. Not unlike the type of chat that all manner of stylists, aestheticians, and sales assistants had tried to have with her since she arrived in London. But it only took one deflected and two unanswered questions for this particular inquisitor to give up. A new record.

Miguel didn't announce his return. On the contrary, he gestured to the painter his intention to remain unnoticed by raising his index finger over his puckered lips. Elsa sat still with her eyes closed while the butterfly wings took shape on her face. Her hands were resting on her lap, one on top of the other. Her back was straight but her neck was free of tension. Could he see a smile resting on her face? Could she be thinking of him? He followed the painter's fingers as they filled in the outlines with vivid colour. And he wished he could paint her—that is, draw a portrait of her.

Miguel had often in the past wished he was a portrait painter; accordingly, he'd also been envious of people who could draw. These thoughts had started early during his photographic career—around the time he transitioned from 35mm film to digital—when he began to have the reoccurring wish of having been born in a time when visually capturing and conveying the essence of a person was only possible through painting or sculpture. The truth that comes from staring at a person for days can't compare to what is perceived in a photography session, where everything is far too rushed. But alas, Miguel had never developed the confidence necessary to hone his drawing skills, for his earliest sketches looked like chicken scratchings not worth the paper they were scribbled on—if his alcoholic and sexually inappropriate art teacher at school was to be taken as an authority on the matter.

Elsa reopened her eyes at the painter's cue, and she instantly burst into laughter at the sight of this lanky panda who was staring at her like she was China's lushest bamboo. Miguel joined her and together they both laughed until tears gathered in their eyes and threatened to smudge their faces. But the painter didn't mind; she was pleased to have spread joy. And although she didn't know it yet, she was lucky to have such a satisfying job.

For the rest of the afternoon, Elsa and Miguel meandered warmly through the zoo, interweaving intellectual talk with immature games. With competing amounts of fascination, they watched the animals and the other visitors watching the animals. They couldn't help zoomorphising the guests any more than they could help anthropomorphising the animals.

Elsa was taking what felt like hundreds of selfies with the animals, mimicking their expression as much as her facial muscles and public persona would allow. And Miguel was busy doing voiceovers. With one eye closed, he would frame an animal between his thumbs and forefingers and deliver remixed renditions of historic speeches: "One small step for man, one giant leap for kangaroo... Ask not what your zoo can do for you, but what you... Five dog years ago..." That sort of thing. He found it amusing, but several nearby post-millennials found it bemusing. After a while, the silly game turned into a serious idea for an exhibition: a series of studio portraits of captive animals with first-person audio narrations instead of the traditional and clichéd text captions.

The last attraction they visited was the insect building. For reasons he didn't care to explain, Miguel decided to sit this one out. But his decision was overruled, and he was forced to tolerate the creepy crawlies—much to Elsa's gleaming delight.

Once outside the zoo, the second thing panda Miguel asked for was food; he was starving. He proposed going back to Vapiano to have the creamy prawn linguini she'd been raving about earlier. Butterfly Elsa offered a better alternative: Chicken Shop in Kentish Town. She also offered a mode of transport and a route: on foot via the canal. It all sounded very quaint and romantic, so he accepted without hesitation.

They walked along the leafy water, through echoing bridges sprayed with street colour, under plaintive droopy trees, past eccentric narrowboats and their owners. When they reached Camden Lock, it was alive with a 5pm Friday swarm of workers celebrating or escaping their week with drink and flirtations. And food, all kinds of wonderfully aromatic foods from all over the world. Miguel was famished. "How much longer?" "Not long. This way." They left the canal and continued on Kentish Town Road. They passed a Nando's along the way. It made him look; it made her chuckle. They walked on: past the station, past the former Art Deco cinema, and almost past the restaurant.

9 THE KISS
(PART 4: RESTAURANT & FEMINISM)

The door to the restaurant was so inconspicuous that Miguel was taken aback when Elsa signalled their arrival. They walked down a narrow flight of stairs to enter the open-plan dining area and kitchen. They didn't have to wait for a table because it was still early for dinner. While they were being seated, Elsa ordered one whole chicken, one side of chips, one side of corn on the cob, one avocado and lettuce salad, and a jar of white wine. Miguel—just a few minutes earlier he'd asked her to pick for both of them due to his ravenous hunger—was impressed by the way she could order off the top of her head, but she humbly rejected that particular compliment in light of the ultra-minimalist menu.

The food came promptly. The rotisserie chicken was succulent and delicious, and its spicy paprika marinade reminded him of Chorizo and her of Morocco. Elsa picked out the breasts while Miguel dived into the thighs, wings, and drumsticks; it was purely a coincidence, albeit a convenient one, that they both preferred different parts. Elsa ate most of the salad—as it turned out Miguel didn't like avocado because of its texture—and joked about this being their last-ever meal together because she couldn't possibly date someone who didn't adore avocados. The corn on the cob was roasted to perfection, but they couldn't finish it; the portion was too big, even for two people. The crinkle cut chips, on the other hand, were finished within seconds. Elsa suggested they hold off ordering another serving so that they could leave some space for dessert, so Miguel had to explain his two independent digestive systems—one for regular food, one for desserts—before ordering another. She laughed at his explanation and felt glad that he was enjoying the food so much.

When they finished their mains, Miguel proposed they come back once a month to celebrate, without specifying what they would be celebrating. Elsa agreed smilingly and warned him that the best was yet to come. She signalled the waiter over and ordered a slice of the apple pie.

A few minutes later, both of them were hovering their faces over the freshly baked dessert. The cinnamon scent was too alluring to ignore. It even reached the adjacent tables. Fellow diners traced it to its source and looked on indiscreetly with tempted faces.

"I'll let you do the honours," he said out of genuine kindness (and without any triteness). He watched the golden pastry crack under her spoon, followed the piece of the pie to the opening of her mouth, then felt it dissolve against her palate.

A cryptic pause. She remained still with her eyes closed. And once she opened them she couldn't speak.

He examined her reaction intently. "Wait. Are you crying?"

"I think I just died and went to heaven," she confessed.

He followed her lead with a mixture of joy and envy.[6]

---

[6] There is a metaphysical significance to this mixture; it is the same recipe of emotions that many summers ago would fill our chests (Miguel's and mine) while trying to keep up with our

And he caught up with her in paradise the moment the sweet-and-sour Bramley apple filling made first contact with his tongue. A moment of silence ensued... It was followed by a sniff. He then pressed the middle knuckle of his index finger against the inner corner of his eye and sniffed again. "Ah fuck, I think I'm crying too..."

They took a moment to evaluate what had just transpired. Some deep shit. To describe this apple pie as life-changing would not be hyperbole, for it was this pie that originally tempted Elsa[7] two years before to break away from her vegan diet—and subsequently, to embrace a more balanced life. The Middle Way.

Naturally, Elsa recalled the conversation she'd had with Maria on that pivotal day. Maria had never seen a face so full of emotion from food—ecstasy and nostalgia and a plethora of other nuanced emotions—but she was not surprised. "You've taken the joy out of food!" she said, to which Elsa replied: "I have taken the joy out of living!" triggering an avalanche of laughter in Maria and an avalanche of revelations in herself.

Elsa and Miguel carried on sharing the dessert, not in silence but certainly without producing any recognisable words. (Neither of them could recognise the other's native-tongue expletives, and moans, while easily understood in any language, aren't really words.) As much as they were enjoying the pie, they were enjoying the experience of being privy to each other's intimate reactions even more.

---

respective older sisters during those long afternoon bike rides.

[7] That the pie is filled with apple is fortuitous, not symbolic.

Miguel offered her the last piece. Elsa borrowed his spoon and, together with hers, used it to collect the last of the pastry along with as much of the middle as possible. Balancing it all, she moved her hand towards his mouth to feed him. "Are you sure?" he asked. She moved her hand even closer. Miguel looked at the spoonful, leaned forward, and engulfed it. When his mouth gave back the empty spoon, Elsa didn't fully retreat it; she rested her elbow on the table and limply balanced it between her index and middle fingers, hovering it in front of his mouth. She noticed his eyeballs roll underneath his eyelids, his tongue sway and relish inside his mouth, and his pronounced Adam's apple rise and rest at the end. He opened his eyes which didn't meet hers; her attention was drawn to his mouth as he licked the sugar off his lips—a reflex. But he missed a small amount of sauce, a golden drop of precious nectar that rested defiantly in the corner of his mouth. That droplet would not be getting away that easily; Elsa dismissed her spoon and reached for it with her dominant hand. Miguel froze. She usurped it from his lips with her thumb, transported it near her mouth, then swallowed it in the most victorious fashion. Then she leaned back, winked at him, and smiled. He fancied this had all taken place in slow motion.

When the bill came, Elsa attempted to pay it all.

Miguel pushed back: "No, no. You've already paid for enough today."

"Enough? And what is enough?"

"The gallery tickets and the zoo tickets."

"Well, you don't know how much—if anything—I paid for the gallery tickets, and I only paid for one zoo ticket, remember?"

"Yeah, but you had that two-for-one voucher..."

"I thought you were a feminist!" She said this with the sole intention of being allowed to pay, and it worked; her quip disarmed him long enough for her to hover her phone over the contactless terminal.

"Would you like a paper receipt?" the waiter asked.

"No, thank you."

"I hope you both enjoyed your meal. Come again soon."

"We'll be back in exactly one month!" she said.

"Perfect, I look forward to it." And with a courteous smile, the waiter returned to the kitchen.

Elsa was getting up from her chair when Miguel suddenly started: "What you said about me not being a feminist if I don't let you pay." She didn't get a chance to explain that she was just teasing because he continued: "I'm not a perfect feminist by any means. I'm still learning."

"None of us are perfect feminists, and I think you're doing fine." But she observed him struggling to fully accept her reassurance, so she sat back down.

"It's just... I don't know. I guess sometimes I worry I may be plateauing with this."

"How so?"

"Well, sexism is such a pervasive phenomenon, but I still don't understand its essence, its roots... You know?"

"Yeah—"

"Like, am I really supposed to believe that it all started seven-thousand years ago with that one evil invention, the plough?"

"I wouldn't worry too much about it. You have the awareness—that's the main thing. If everyone had that we'd be at parity already... So, shall we?"

The night and the cold surprised them when they exited the basement restaurant. Time had flown by and the temperature had fallen disproportionately. Elsa hurriedly zipped up her insufficient jacket; Miguel didn't have one, so he just squeezed his chest and blew a few hot breaths into his cupped hands. Without deliberation they agreed to head towards Kentish Town station and maybe stop in a pub along the way if they could find one that wasn't too rowdy on a Friday night. Each had their reason: Elsa wanted a fruity Gin and Tonic to rinse off the nagging guilt of not having spent the afternoon studying, while Miguel wanted an Old Fashioned to curtail a growing inhibition that he could neither escape nor explain. Also, they were both a little tipsy from the dinner wine.

She put her arm through his for body warmth, and together they set off. As soon as they did, Elsa noticed and highlighted his loose shoelace. Miguel knelt down beside her and began tying his Yeezys. Tying one meant tying the other because he hated feeling different pressures on his feet. She used this timeout to check for Overground train times on her phone. She saw several notifications, but she only paid attention to one recent WhatsApp from Maria asking her how the date was going. This question, timestamped 19:45, almost five hours later than the time Elsa said she would be home by, and its annoying implication that Maria knew her better than she knew herself, triggered a moment of emotional self-awareness. Sharply, a spark inside her chest sent a fiery sensation of affection roaring through her torso. She felt it spread rampantly through her limbs and neck—too fast for her to contain—until it reached her feet and hands and face, and these began to contort. Miguel finished tying his trainers and jumped up as if to make up for lost time when he noticed her lost in tense introspection. He called out to her. She completely missed his words but trustfully hooked on to their intonation to slingshot back to the outside world.

"Come here."

He obeyed her command with a nervous step.

She hugged him, inhaled from his neck, and exhaled her frustrations through a loud growl. Her next inhale invited his body to mould around hers.

He wrapped his arms around her waist and raised them until they locked against hers. Then he lifted her off her feet until her neck met his lips. There he smelled her under the jawline and lost himself in her. That was the first time the profundity of his feelings took a conscious form in his soul. His uncountable emotions condensed into a single thought and three monosyllables spawned. He felt an almost overwhelming urge to tell her, but his fear overruled him. "Your smell... it's intoxicating," was as far as he was allowed to stray. He lowered her in the same way that he had raised her.

"Gosh, you're surprisingly strong! Especially for someone who doesn't work out."

"Yeah, but only for like the first three minutes."

She made an em sound with overt sexual overtones.

But the joke was lost on him because all of a sudden he was deep in thought. His focus seemed to have drifted to an imaginary point some twenty meters under the ground. Then, in a single blink, his focus snapped back to the surface where it erratically bounced from object to object until it inevitably landed on Elsa. Miguel felt as if he might have unearthed a revelatory thought: "Men are, on average, physically stronger than women, right? And nearly every culture in the world is patriarchal, right? So maybe the root of sexism is the fact that men are physically stronger?"

"Elaborate."

"That's it."

"That's it?"

"That's all I've got so far!"

"Haha! Okay. Well, I don't think one thing inevitably leads to the other. Have you heard of the Bonobo chimpanzee? They didn't have them in this zoo, but they're our closest relative."

"Yes, I have."

"Well, their males are also bigger and physically stronger than their females, but their communities are completely matriarchal."

"Oh, well, there goes that theory then. Haha!"

"Not at all! I believe sex dimorphism was the first of three phenomena that, combined, paved the way for the patriarchal society we now find ourselves in."

"And the other two?"

"Monogamy, which led to the over-sexualisation of women; and sedentary civilisations, which allowed us to accumulate surplus goods."

Miguel moved his head—something between a nod and a tilt.

"Let me explain. Our reproductive biology is different, so our mating priorities are different. Women are more discriminate than men when it comes to reproduction because they have more to lose, because the parental investment of a mother is higher than that of a father: a minimum of ten months between successful pregnancies versus as little as ten minutes between ejaculations.

Accordingly, our mating instincts have evolved differently. Men's reproductive instincts drive them to inseminate as many seemingly fertile women as possible, while women's reproductive instincts drive them to the man that promises the strongest chance of survival for their offspring." She glanced at him; he was still listening, rather attentively in fact, so she continued: "Now, these blunt instincts may be powerful, but they are by no means the only ones. Humans are also attracted to other, more nuanced characteristics—the most relevant of which, at least as it pertains to the establishment of the patriarchy, being monogamy. Consider monogamy as a highly desirable trait for a mating partner. (And I'll explain in a moment why that is the case, but for now please take it as a given.) Women's desire for an exclusive mating partner pits them against other women for the attention of the most eligible bachelors. And, for better or worse, the evolutionarily stable strategy that emerged in this competitive environment was for women to put on a display of their most attractive trait: fertility, the promise of many offspring. You know, full lips, big breasts, wide hips, and a thin waist—because a pregnant woman is the least fertile of them all!"

"So you're saying that it was women's own expectations of monogamy which led them to over-sexualise their own body?"

"Basically."

He let it sink in.

"By the way, I'm speaking purely from a biological perspective here. I'm not making any moral judgements. Let me just make that perfectly clear. Also, I don't want to seem heteronormative with all this, but the reality is that until we invent same-sex reproduction any discussion about the genetic evolution of our species will, by design, be limited to heterosexual relationships only."

"Of course. And what about men? How did their desire for monogamy affect their behaviour?"

"It didn't alter men's behaviour towards each other. Men carried on competing for access to the best women in the same way that they had previously competed for access to the most women: by fighting. However, it did alter their behaviour towards women. It gave rise to all kinds of societal repressions of female sexuality, from shaming to lynching."

"Damn... Doesn't seem to have been a very positive invention this monogamy thing. How did it even catch on if it caused so much harm to society?"

"Oh, yes! I said I would explain that. There are two dominant theories for the spread of monogamy, and they both assert that men were the drivers."

"Really?"

"Yeah. The most popular theory claims that men demanded monogamy mainly as a way of ensuring that their partner's offspring were actually theirs since there was no way for them to continuously supervise their whole harem. The other theory claims that men demanded lifelong monogamy mainly as a way of safeguarding their offspring against infanticide from rivals."

"Infanticide?" he asked with raised eyebrows as if in disbelief that ancient men could ever have performed such an atrocity. But even contemporary men have been known to commit all types of -cides.

"Yes, first infanticide and then monogamy! I keep saying it: men, not money, are the root of all evil!"

This made him laugh.

"Actually, in the interest of completeness and fairness, I should probably say that there is a third theory, and it asserts that it was women who demanded monogamy from their partner because of their need for assistance with childrearing. But that theory is not widely accepted, and it's more likely that paternal assistance emerged as a side effect of monogamy."

"I agree. Just because a mother needs help with the baby, it doesn't necessarily mean that she needs it from the father, or even from a blood relative for that matter."

"Indeed."

"Okay, so sexual dynamorphism and monogamy are the first two pieces of the puzzle."

"Dimorphism."

"Yes, that too. Haha! So where does the third piece, sedentary civilisations, fit in?"

"For millions of years, prehistoric humans only owned what they could carry because they lived in small nomadic tribes. Unfortunately (or fortunately, depending on your opinion) that all changed a few thousand years ago with the rise of sedentary civilisations. Both men and women started accumulating wealth, but the reproductive differences I mentioned earlier gave men a stronger drive, or to be more precise, a stronger incentive to do so." She darted a glance at him to make sure he was still following.

He was: "Because a rich man can sustain a harem, but no matter how rich a woman gets she can still only give birth about once per year?"

"Exactly."

"So as men began accumulating wealth they used their increased power to become more polygamous?"

"Yup..."

"But I'm guessing they still demanded monogamy from their women for the same reasons as before: to make sure they weren't bringing up somebody else's child, and to keep their children out of harm's way?"

"You got it. Oh, and the last thing I should mention—and this is crucial—is that men didn't stop being selective in their mating partners once they started accumulating wealth. Unlike stags on a hill or elephant seals on a beach, men in early settlements and later on in towns and cities had physical access to literally thousands of women, but none except the most powerful Ghenkis Khan types had the resources to protect and support all of them. And that's why men maintained a degree of selectivity, preferring to compete for the women that satisfied their reproductive instincts and complied with their behavioural expectations, and why single women continued to compete against each other for male attention by displaying their beautiful fertility and by complying with those male expectations."

They stopped at a crossing. They stood shoulder-to-shoulder with the back of their hands almost rubbing. Elsa looked at Miguel and saw a man that reunited her with so many lost reveries, too many to keep in check. Miguel looked both ways and saw a sliver of opportunity to cross and automatically grabbed her by the hand and ran. She screamed and once they had reached the other side called him crazy for it, and together they laughed. But it wasn't until the adrenaline had died down that he became aware of the fact that they were walking holding hands—for the first time. She felt his surprise and found it amusing, and she flirted with the idea of making a joke out of it but decided against it because she didn't want to risk losing this rare physical connection. So instead, she deflected with a cute thought triggered by a sock monkey in a tea advert on the side of a red double-decker bus.

10 THE KISS
(PART 5: PUB & MUSIC)

They entered a pleasing pub and headed upstairs in search of the cosiest corner. Elsa went to the ladies while Miguel waited. Because of his GoldenEye past, he used this time to devise in his mind several increasingly unrealistic emergency exit strategies. As soon as Elsa returned, Miguel went to the bar, via the gents, to get that Old Fashioned and Gin and Tonic. She used this time to appreciate the pub's hygge interior design and to upload a video story of it. #bullandgatenw5

He came back with their drinks. She thanked him; he welcomed her. They clinked glasses and took their first sips. She asked him if he'd ever tasted hers. He didn't think so, so she insisted he try some right away.

"Wow, this is fucking amazing!"

"I know, right?"

"What is it?"

"What do you mean? You ordered it!" She tasted it just in case. He hadn't got her order wrong; it was unmistakably Brockmans.

"Yeah, no, I mean, what's in it?"

"Oh! Well, it's got juniper, berries, liquorice... Er, what else? Orange peel, cinnamon—"

"Damn, sounds like a dessert!"

"Haha! Yeah, I guess it does. But I love it. It's my favourite."

"I like a woman who knows and enjoys her food and drink."

"I know, right? I actually can't trust people who don't take their food and drink seriously. For instance, I have this friend, Enia, who for months kept trying to take me to some Chinese buffet that, she claimed, had all-you-can-eat lobster for ten pounds..."

"Ten pounds?!"

"Yup, go figure! Now obviously I couldn't have her lie to my face, so we argued about it until she caved and conceded that maybe it hadn't been lobster, maybe it had been crab claws..."

"Still though. All-you-can-eat crab claws for a tenner?"

"I know. Trust me, I know. So anyway, a few months later she finally managed to trick me into going to that hideous restaurant."

"How did she trick you?"

"She guilt-tripped me! She organised an I'm-moving-away dinner and chose that restaurant. I couldn't say no."

"Ah, clever fox!"

"But anyway, guess what? The infamous lobster-tail-turned-crab-claws turned out to be those cheap surimi nuggets—you know, the ones that are covered in golden breadcrumbs and have a little decorative pincer sticking out the side like this." And she traced one on the dark wood table using her index finger and some dew scooped from the outside of her balloon glass.

Miguel laughed.

"No, no, no, but that's not even the funny part. What's really shocking is that when we first walked to the hot food counter to check who'd been right all along, once we're both standing in front of the same greasy chafing dish full of deep-fried nuggets—me already rolling my eyes like, 'Really?'—she actually turned to me and with her face all smug said: 'See? I told you so!'"

Miguel laughed even harder.

Elsa enjoyed it.

For the rest of the round, they continued sharing entertaining anecdotes. Spoken words enter the body as vibrations. Some of those vibrations are metamorphosed in the ear canal into electrical signals and then transported to the brain to be cognised as speech. But some of those vibrations enter the body raw through the epidermis and diffuse into every non-baryonic particle of our inner form. This is how plants hear. This is how humans grow to feel, trust, and love one another.

They decided to stay for a second round. Miguel took both empty glasses and made his way to the bar. He clawed his short tumbler from above with his left hand, using only his fingertips, and cupped her balloon glass in his right palm, lodging its stem between his middle and ring fingers like a rudder. As he walked, he stifled the natural swinging motion of his arms for fear of smashing the glasses. And as he went down the stairs, he observantly placed one foot in front of the other for fear of falling. All in all, the journey to the bar took him a non-negligible amount of concentration, and it was on noticing this that he became aware of how tipsy he was.

The bartender thanked him for returning the glasses, put them in a grey plastic crate, and began making two Brockmans Gin and Tonics in clean glasses. Miguel never understood why bar staff always refuse to reuse glasses, but he held back this question (for the umpteenth time) and

promised himself to ask it next time it arose.[8] The
bartender, a boisterous Aussie, struck up a conversation as
he made the drinks: "How's the date going, mate?" Date.
That was quite observant of him, but frankly Miguel hadn't
really thought about it. "That's not bad, mate. Means
you've been enjoying the moment." It was a fair point. "Just
make sure you don't get so caught up in the moment that
you miss the bigger picture—and the opportunity. You gotta
strike while the iron's hot, mate!" Miguel laughed out loud
and told the barman he would see what he could do.

* * *

Elsa surveyed Miguel's gait as he made his way to the bar
for the second round. Somehow it seemed unique,
although she was unable to pinpoint why. A parent penguin
returning to its colony after hunting in the ocean can find
its young among a vast crèche of wailing chicks. This and
other similarly random thoughts prompted Elsa to take
stock of the alcohol she had consumed so far. "Let's see,
two glasses of white wine and one Brockmans. Det är
okej." She reached into her regular Carmex pocket in her
belt bag, reverse-scooped some out with the outside of her
fingernail, and applied it liberally on her lips. "Plus the one
that's coming! Ah, skit! Och vad är klockan?" She checked
on her wristwatch. It was 21:30. "Ah, skit! Already?" She
put the Carmex back, but in her jacket pocket. "Damn, I
really need to go home after this drink." She had to wake
up early and get back to her studying. "But what about
Miguel?" She was worried he might ask her to go back to

---

[8] If only I could communicate with Miguel, I would be able to
explain to him why bar staff always refuse to reuse glasses.

his. "I hope he won't feel rejected. I might have to explain it to him." But she was reluctant to talk about her upcoming viva examination on Tuesday for fear of talking it into existence. "Or maybe I should just go back to his for a little bit and then get a cab home. After all, it's only 21:30." She reached into her bag for her Carmex, but it wasn't there. So she searched for it pocket by pocket until she found it. And it wasn't until the minty moisturising balm touched her already minty moisturised lips that she felt the déjà vu. "Vad fan gör jag?" She pressed her lips together and rubbed them against each other. She put the Carmex back—in its proper place this time—just as Miguel returned with the drinks.

"Were you talking to yourself?"

"No..." Any blush from her mild embarrassment was masked by the blush from the evening's alcohol and the blush from the day's sun; nevertheless, she still tried to conceal it by hiding her face behind her (transparent) drink. "By the way, we should probably call it a date—call it a date?—call it a day after this one." She took her first sip of her second Gin and Tonic. "Mmm... This is so good! Thanks."

"You're welcome. And yeah, it's been a long day—day?—date! All days have the same length. Haha!" He took his first sip. "Oh yeah, this is really good!"

"Did you get the same as me this time?"

"Yes I did. By the way, thank you for introducing me to Brockmans. I'd actually never had it before."

"It's my favourite."

"And thank you for making this the best date of my life."

"What?!"

"Wait. Did I say 'date' or 'day'?"

"Date."

"Okay. Then, yes, thank you for it!"

"But... has this really been the best date of your life?"

"Oh, absolutely! I couldn't have had a better one. On top of the crazy gallery and the fun zoo and the amazing food, the company has been nothing short of perfect!"

"Aw, well I'm flattered," she said. "And I really wish it didn't have to end but—"

"But I imagine we'll see each other again soon, no? I mean, I hope so anyway... Would you like to see me again? I would like to see you again. And you?"

She laughed. (It's not a thin line between cute and cringe; thankfully, it's more of a broad spectrum.) "Yes, of course I would."

They both smiled, first at each other, then shyly. Then Elsa took another dissimulating long sip, which Miguel mirrored.

"You know, you're very different from all of the other creeps that message me on Instagram. It's very refreshing."

"Wait, did you just call me a creep?"

"Nooo!" And she grabbed his hand as if asking for forgiveness. "It was a compliment!"

"Yeah, a back-handed compliment, perhaps!"

"No! I simply meant that you're thoughtful and insightful and—"

"That's great. I'm going toilet."

"Oi!"

"No, I actually need to go."

"Okay, but hurry up, I want to finish what I was saying."

He walked away, and she followed him with her eyes.

"Okay so, what were you saying?"

"One minute, I actually need to go too."

"Okay. Go, go, go!"

She got up fast and power-walked to the toilet, obliviously absorbing his gaze until she was out of sight.

First thing she did when she returned was to ask him to crack her back.

"To what?"

"You've never done it before?"

"No," he replied. "And I'm not sure I even know what you mean by that."

"Oi, don't have such a dirty mind!"

"What?"

"Here, I'll show you how it's done. Get up. Lock your hands together intertwining your fingers, like this. Put them behind your neck, like this. Okay, turn around. Damn, you're tall! Er... I know! Let me just stand on this armchair, so I can squat and lift you properly."

"What?!"

"What."

"You're going to lift me?"

"Yeah, that's the whole point. You have to lift me. But I have to do it to you first because it's almost impossible to describe the movement. Okay, so you're going to wrap your arms around me, putting my elbows in your palms, like this. My elbows have to be together the whole time you lift me—that's very important. I'm going to lock my fingers to help me lift you, but you might be strong enough that you don't need to. And then you lift. Lift! Not yank, not bounce, not shake, just lift. Okay?"

"Yup. Lift."

"You got it. But as you lift you're going to squeeze my elbows towards my chest, like this. And you're going to push your chest against my back, like this. Together your hands and chest will squeeze my rib cage, like this. Now, did you get all that?"

"Yeah, I think I got it."

"And do you have any questions?"

"No. Let me try it on you now."

"Wait, I haven't done it to you yet. This is the best part! Okay, relax." She did a test mini-lift. "No, but you really have to relax because this doesn't work unless you're relaxed."

"How can I relax?"

"Look, Miguel, do you trust me?"

He read more into that question than was intended. He was fully ready to give her his trust. "Yes, I trust you," he declared. And he closed his eyes and completely relaxed inside her arms.

Most learning occurs through visual or auditory channels, but Elsa was teaching Miguel the back-cracking technique kinaesthetically, evoking an empathetic energy which usually resides dormant in most of us, the kind that a blind person might feel when being taught how to dance. Miguel felt this rare energy flow through his body. Then a burdensome weight—time itself—escaped him, leaving in its wake an enduring lightness of being. In this state, his sense of self diffused. And for a fleeting moment, Elsa engulfed him until she became his world. But before he could catch that moment, before he could name it and synthesise it and store it as a memory, she lifted and squeezed him and a dozen consecutive thoracic vertebrae cracked.

"Yes!" she screamed in satisfaction at her achievement.

She hopped down from the armchair, turned him around, and asked him: "Did you love it?"

Miguel was in shock. "I feel like I've been baptised," he said. And he didn't directly answer her question, but yes he did love it (and everything about her).

"Okay, now I want you to do the same thing to me."

Miguel skilfully retraced the steps of the move exactly as she had taught him. He lifted and squeezed her and felt that striking cracking sensation from the external perspective. And on that high note, they decided to head home.

Elsa ordered an Uber with a few terse commands to her virtual assistant who was nevertheless happy to oblige. ETA was two minutes, so they had to down the last of their Brockmans. Elsa couldn't down hers, and Miguel did but not without provoking a searing brain freeze. They made their way out. Miguel opened the front door of the pub for her, like the true gentleman that he'd never been. As she walked through it, he stared at her ass and got extremely turned on again by the way it filled out her jeans. He'd carried a semi pretty much permanently since she'd wiped off her butterfly face, but now he was packing an erection so hard it almost hurt him.[9] To make it less glaringly obvious, he stealthily rearranged his penis—tucked it diagonally under his belt—as he walked through the door behind her.

Once inside the car, Elsa confirmed with the driver her identity and the directions she had entered in the app,

---

[9] Do not be alarmed. This was not a case of priapism. Miguel was perfectly healthy.

directions to her house in Kensal Green via Miguel's in Maida Vale. The driver pulled away, and she sank into her seat and relaxed—that special relaxation that is bestowed exclusively by a moving vehicle: a car, a pram, your mother's rocking arms...

Elsa ran her hands over her jeans, from the top of her thighs to her knees then along the side of her thighs to her hips. The friction of the denim against her palms generated a tantalising soft hiss. She shifted her weight left then right to sit on her hands. Miguel imagined them enviously. She locked her elbows, lifting her shoulders into a shrug and triggering a deep inhale. She abruptly released one hand from underneath her bum just in time to cover the yawn that ensued. Miguel followed suit and yawned too. This made her smile.

Elsa asked the driver if she could play some music. Of course she could. She connected via Bluetooth to the car's speakers and played In Those Jeans by Ginuwine. That opening guitar riff stunned Miguel and left him grappling with his short-term memory, unable to trace with any confidence a partition between thought and speech. Noticing his confusion, she leaned in close to his face and whispered spookily: "I can read your thoughts!" His fearfulness made her laugh hard. "Hahaha! I guess you didn't realise you were humming it to yourself literally a few seconds ago, huh?" Unable to resist that embarrassed face of his, she slid closer to him, grabbed his arm, and rested her head on his shoulder. They stayed this way listening to the song, feeling a complex mixture of nostalgia and hope, her with her eyes closed, him staring out the window at the London night.

As the song reached the bridge, Miguel asked if he

could make a request.

"Of course."

"You Are Everything by—"

"Oh my god, that is literally my jam!"

"You like Dru Hill, yeah?"

She found the song within seconds and played it without waiting for the current one to finish. That opening acoustic guitar, that subsequent drum kit, and that #Last night we had an argument# stirred her soul and twisted her face much like that apple pie had done a few of hours earlier.

When she finally emerged from her daydream, shortly after the beginning of the first chorus, she belatedly answered his question with a stern look on her face and his blameless wrist in her hand. "Are you fucking kidding me? I love Dru Hill! I love all slow jams: R. Kelly, Donell Jones, Boyz II Men, Jodeci—oh my god, Jodeci. I'm sooo gonna play them next!"

"Haha! I like your style."

"Listen, if you're really serious about your slow jams then we might just get along."

"Oh yeah?"

"Yeah... This," and she traced an ellipse in the air between them, "might actually work."

Her first reference to themselves as a couple. He couldn't even try to contain the inordinate smile raging all over his face.

"And if you're into your '90s West Coast Gansta Rap, specifically G-funk, we might just have to elope tonight."

His smile swelled up to inhuman proportions until it burst.

"Oi, don't laugh! The G-funk era was the bomb: Nate Dogg, Warren G, Luniz, Blackstreet, Bone Thugs-N—"

He kept on laughing.

"Why is that funny? Actually, don't answer that." She didn't want to get into a race debate.

"You're too fucking adorable!"

"Whatever..."

He managed to restrain his laughter so he could explain: "Please don't get me wrong. It's not about your skin colour or anything. It's more of a culture thing. I mean, Finland and Cali are so far apart that I just never expected... But no, I like that you like G-funk. I like it too."

"Yes, it's true that most of the people in Finland wouldn't listen to '90s rap. But when I was a little girl—ten or eleven—one of my mum's friends who had a very eclectic taste in music gave me this G-funk compilation CD for my birthday, and I played it non-stop until I actually ended up knowing most of the lyrics by heart."

"And with your brain, I bet you still know them!"

"Ooh, you've just given me a brilliant idea! Have you ever been to Hip Hop Karaoke?"

"I think I tried to go in once a couple of years ago, but the queue was too long so we ended up going somewhere else."

"What time is it now, can we still make it? Wait, damn it! It's Friday today, isn't it? Ah, knull! Oh well, it'll have to be next week then..."

"Haha! Okay. Sure."

"Sure? You pinky-promise?" And she raised her pinky in front of his face.

"Well, let's talk about it tomorrow when we're sober and once we've checked—"

"Ah, you're no fun!" And she pushed him away jovially.

And he poked her on her side.

And she jumped—Elsa was extremely ticklish—and retaliated with a hard, twisting pinch to the skin on his triceps.

"Ouch! Domestic violence! I could sue you for that."

"Hey…" Her tone was suddenly different somehow.

"What?"

"Do you still have that bottle of whiskey that you wanted to give me at my birthday party? The one you said you would keep for our next date."

"The Quiet Man. Yes, I do. It's at home. Why?"

"And your housemate, Juno, is he also at home?"

"Hugo. I don't know. I can check. Why?" He took out his phone to message him.

"Find out and let me know. If he's not home, or if he doesn't mind, maybe I can come in to have quick a taste of this Quiet Man. I want to see what all the fuss is all about."

Miguel took this suggestion very seriously because it looked as if Elsa might actually be down to fuck—that second-date luck—so he tried to play it cool. "Alright, let me see what he's up to…" Miguel was a good actor. "Oh, looks like I have a few messages from him already… And a few missed calls too, actually… Okay, he says there's a few peeps coming round for a drink tonight."

"Ooh, sounds like a party!"

"Nah, knowing him it's probably just a little gathering. A weed smoking session followed by a paranoid discussion of the hottest conspiracy theories: Chemtrails, Russia's Troll Army, Big Pharma, that sort of thing… Would you like to join?"

"Well, when you put it like that! Haha!"

"Ha! I guess you're right. That doesn't sound very appetising, does it?"

"I was joking. It doesn't sound all bad. Actually, sometimes I find listening to people with colourful views quite refreshing—the scientific method can get a little bit drab after a while... So maybe next time I'll join, but not today. I'm too tired to meet new people now, and I wouldn't want your friends to think I'm unfriendly. Us Finns already have a bad reputation for being cold!"

"Yeah, I get it."

"So I think I'll just go home and crash."

"That's fine. No worries."

"But if you're not busy this weekend maybe we can hang out?"

"Yeah, sure, that would be nice."

"Actually, if Hugh's not busy—and if he's single, and good looking, and interesting, and overall just super amazing, like you—then maybe we can introduce him to Maria. I'll ask her what she's up to. I don't think she's got plans this weekend."

"Hugo," he repeated, hopefully for the last time, "is all of the above, although obviously not as much as me. Haha!"

"Hahaha! Obviously! Who is, right?"

"But yeah, double date. That could be interesting—or disastrous. Haha! Either way, let's make it happen."

"Awesome!"

And once they finished laughing she rested her head on his shoulder and he rested his head on hers, and they locked arms and interlocked fingers, and they sat wordlessly in this position for the rest of the journey. Their vocal silence didn't separate them, and their hands didn't join them—their connection transcended their senses. A week ago, neither of them would have even contemplated this type of emotional intimacy, but something inside them had changed during this date, and now they were no longer afraid.

The car decelerated smoothly until it came to a standstill. The driver announced their arrival at the first destination once it became evident that neither of the napping passengers had noticed it.

"Oh, we're here already?" Miguel ducked to get a better look out the windows—not quite incredulity, just an innocuous habit. "Well, Elsa, once again, thank you for everything, really. I've had an incredible day."

"Me too!" she said with the most painfully beautiful smile.

He unbuckled his seatbelt. "Message me when you get home."

"Yes, I will. And I'll speak to Maria and let you know about tomorrow—or Sunday."

He placed his hand on the door handle, but he didn't open the door. He turned to her once more, but by then she was busy taking out her phone and switching on its flashlight.

"Have you got everything?" she asked him as she scanned the floor and ran her hand along the grooves of the backseat in search of a non-existent lost item.

He shifted out of the way of her flashlight until he somehow ended up outside the car looking in. Regret, or rather that instinct before regret, started to jab at him. After all these hours he had missed his chance to kiss her. He patted his pockets theatrically. "Yes, I have everything. Goodnight, Elsa." He waved her goodbye, closed the door, and tapped the car on the roof twice.

The car moved no more than a few decimetres before stopping abruptly. Miguel heard her shout his name from inside the car and went to open the door to ask her what was up but took a step back when he saw her getting out.

"Come here," she said, taking a bold step towards his face. "I want a kiss."

11 HUGO'S SIGNATURE CAKE

Miguel walked to his front door and rang the bell. He had keys, but he chose to announce his arrival this way. Hugo opened the door and welcomed him with a big papa bear hug. He was high as a kite. He asked him how his date had gone and, without waiting for an answer, told him about the little surprise he had for him.

Stephany was a petite Brazilian girl with overflowing levels of energy, an unquenchable thirst for alcohol, and an as-yet unfed curiosity for black guys. She had a cute face and a curvy figure, but the thing that instantly attracted Miguel to her—apart from his blue balls courtesy of Elsa's momentous parting kiss just a few seconds earlier—was her dyed red hair, which he took as a sign of spontaneity, maybe restlessness, hopefully insecurity.

Miguel had barely finished greeting all the guests when Hugo—accompanied by Thaís, his reliable fuckfriend and Stephany's older cousin—pulled him aside and prodded him into action: "Bro, what are you doing? That girl is a penalty kick! And when you get granted a penalty kick, you don't question the referee's decision, you don't deliberate or time waste, you do what you were trained to do: you step up, shoot, and score!" It's not clear why Thaís condoned this uneven match, let alone why she seconded Hugo's pearls of wisdom, but her opinion by that point was redundant because Miguel's only remaining reservation was Stephany's age; however, Thaís assured him that she was perfectly legal. Although, arguably, the adjective 'barely' (which contains even fewer syllables) would have been more descriptive.

Evidently, Miguel didn't need much in the way of persuading, in spite of his earlier date. He cast all that Elsa aside, served himself a slice of chocolate cake, poured himself a White Russian, and focused on the task at hand. After surreptitiously examining the situation from a distance, he manufactured an opportunity to talk to Stephany one-on-one. A little small talk—that's all it took really.

Stephany had three skeuomorphic tattoos on display: a clock and a compass on each forearm and a large marionette across her back. These served as the perfect conversation starter. The first two tattoos symbolised the ideas that time is precious and that no matter how lost you feel you can always find your way home, respectively. The meaning of the third tattoo was for her to know and him to find out, apparently. Miguel found out approximately three hours later. The marionette symbolised her predilection for being manhandled during sex to a level which a psychologist could only diagnose as masochistic.

Five days, six unanswered calls, and seventeen pairs of WhatsApp blue ticks later—once she'd been forced to understand his totally uninterested position through a firm-but-fair message which fulfilled her desire for closure with one so airtight that it made her recall the proverb 'Be careful what you wish for!' with a grimace—Stephany would go on to claim that Miguel had taken advantage of her because he knew that she was out of it from Hugo's cake, which everyone had failed to inform her was laced to the brim with cannabis.

12 THE DOUBLE DATE
(PART 1: DINNER)

"Alright, act cool tonight. I'm tryna impress this chick."

"What d'you mean you're tryna... Oh, shit, you ain't banged her yet? Bro, you're losing your skills."

"Shut your mouth! I ain't losing nothing."

"You sure about that? Cos you been chasing this girl for over a month. Whatever happened to your tried-and-tested technique for fucking bitches by the second date?"

"I've only known her for three weeks. And actually, I got a kiss on our last date, which was our second date."

"Pah! A kiss, he says... When I first met you, you could get laid with any bitch you wanted. These days, you have to resort to spiking underage girls to get some pussy!"

"Fuck off! She wasn't underage. And I didn't spike anyone. It was you who made that cake, not me."

"Don't even try and shift the blame on me, Mr Humbert. You were all over that nymphet like, 'Come here, girl. Eat some of this chocolate cake. You like chocolate, don't ya? Yeah, I can tell...'"

"Dickhead!"

"Hahaha! Bro, why d'you even go for these low-self-esteem-having bitches, anyway? Is it a penis-size issue?"

"You wanna see my dick, bro? Is that it?"

"Nah, bro, I'm good."

"Well then. And stop calling women bitches!"

"What the fuck, so now you're the only one that's

allowed to disrespect women?"

"When do I ever fucking disrespect women?"

"Pah! With a straight face, he asks that... Never mind, clearly today's not the day for your intervention."

"Bro, if you fuck this up for me..."

"Bro, are you questioning my wingmanness? wingmanhood? wingmanity? wingmanicity? wing—"

"Alright, enough."

"You know what? Let's light one up. You seem a little uptight. You gotta loosen up a little before we get there."

"I don't know, bro. Elsa has very liberal views, and Maria seems like she probably smokes herself. But maybe we shouldn't, just in case."

"Just in case what?"

"I don't know, bro..."

"Bro, I'm lighting up. You're acting mad strange right now and it's freaking me out—and it'll probably freak them out too."

"I just don't wanna go in there all smelling of weed, you know? And their flat is just around the corner."

"Bro, it's like this: Elsa will probably respect you for exercising your right to self-determination, and if this Maria chick isn't smoking up right now, she's probably caressing and singing to her marijuana plants."

"Yeah, you're probably right. And if we're lucky they'll smell it on us and suggest we all smoke up together."

"That's the spirit! And then we can all have an orgy. Haha!"

"Stop chatting shit and light the weed up."

"This is it. Hold on let me ring her, cos she told me the intercom isn't working or something... Oi, what you doing?"

"Bro, it's open."

"Oh, alright. I'll hang up then. Come, I think it's this way."

"By the way, where are those LED cats?"

"What LED cats? Oh... Nah, that wasn't her house last Friday. She had her birthday party somewhere else. Hold on. I think this is their flat. Yeah, this is it."

"Wait!"

"Why?"

"Just a few last-minute touches. Wanna make sure I look proper, innit. Mint?"

"What, so you can smell of minty weed, yeah?"

"Yooo, you've just given me a banging idea for a new hybrid!"

"You're nuts."

"Carmex?"

"Bro..."

"What, you wanna go inside with those ashy lips, yeah?"

"Ashy? What ashy? Give me that!"

"Well, it looks like you two might need a minute. Perhaps I should come back later."

"Oh! Hi, Elsa. We were just about to ring the doorbell."

"No need, we could hear you squabbling from inside. Also, you called me by accident."

"Oh shit! It didn't hang up?"

"Hi, I'm Elsa. You must be Hugo."

"Yes, I am. Pleasure to make your acquaintance. I've heard so many good things about you."

"Pleasure to make your acquaintance? Bro..."

"What? I've spotted a lot of encouraging signs these past few weeks, so it really is a pleasure to meet the source of all that positive change."

"For fuck's sake..."

"Miguel, behave. The pleasure is all mine, Hugo. Please, come in."

"Shoes off?"

"Yes, please. Although you can wear these grey slippers if you like. They're for our guests."

"What a splendid idea! This way you keep the dirt out of the house, and your guests' feet stay nice and—"

"Elsa, where's Maria?"

"She's just popped into her room for a moment. She'll be out in just a second. Make yourselves comfortable in the living room while I go get you something to drink. What would you like? Maria made some—"

"I'll have what everyone else is having. I just need to pop to the toilet."

"Yes, of course. Er, it's the first door on the left... So, Hugo—oh, by the way, I'm absolutely terrible with names so let me know if I'm not pronouncing it right."

"No, no, you said it perfectly. And as for the drink, we brought something."

"Oh, awesome!"

"But we have to prepare it first."

"Sure. And do you need me to put it in the fridge in the meantime?"

"You have ice?"

"Yeah, Maria bought loads."

"Then, no. We can just keep it here in that case."

"Sure."

"So, did you get up to much this weekend? The weather's been gorgeous, hasn't it?"

"Yes, it really has! Friday I spent it with Miguel. I don't

know if he told you, but we went to a weird gallery, then the zoo, and then we had some food."

"Oh, that's right. Yes, he did tell me."

"So that was good, but since then I've just been holed up in my room working non-stop."

"Miguel tells me you're studying a PhD in, Environmental Economics?"

"Yes. Well, Ecological Economics—but close enough."

"Oh, sorry. I must have misheard him or misremembered him."

"It's fine. Most people make the same mistake. I suspect most people think the two names are interchangeable."

"And please forgive my ignorance, but what is the difference between the two?"

"No, it's not ignorance. The difference is rather nuanced, and we practitioners have perhaps not done a good enough job of communicating it. But in a nutshell, it's all about hierarchy. In environmental economics, the environment is subservient to the economy, whereas in ecological economics, the economy is delimited by our ecosystem—planet earth."

"Interesting!"

"What's interesting?"

"She was just telling me about her PhD."

"Oh yeah. This one's a proper brainiac, bro. Watch out!"

"Thank you, Miguel. What about you, Hugo? Tell me about your life. What gets you up in the mornings and what keeps you up at night?"

"Trust me. You don't wanna know..."

"Let's see. I'm a part-time landlord... and also a part-time purveyor of controlled substances for medicinal and/or recreational purposes."

"Ah, so you're a drug dealer. How delightful! I guess that explains why you're so couth. Haha!"

"Who's a drug dealer?"

"Hi, Maria."

"Hi, Miguel. What did I miss?"

"This is my housemate Hugo."

"Hi, Hugo. Nice to meet you."

"Hi, Maria. Likewise."

"Maria, Hugo was just telling me what he does for a living. Interestingly, his business concerns span property and pharmaceuticals."

"Well, in that case, Hugo isn't just my housemate—he's also my pharmacist. Haha!"

"And best friend!"

"Oi!"

"What? You told me he was your best friend. I didn't know it was supposed to be a secret!"

"Yeah, well, you don't have to say it in front of him. He's gonna get a big head now."

"Aww, you two are so cute when you argue."

"Don't worry, bro. I know how you really feel about me. By the way Maria, your Thai green curry smells absolutely delicious."

"How did you know? Did Elsa tell you what was for dinner?"

"No, I didn't say anything!"

"Whoa, are you making the same curry that you made at the birthday party? Because that curry was the bomb!"

"Elsa didn't tell me. I recognise the unmistakable aroma."

"Interesting... Right, who wants a drink?"

"Maria, why don't you take Hugo to the kitchen. He says they brought a drink that needs making."

"Yes, I thought transporting it ready-made would be more troublesome than making it here."

"Of course, come with me. These two lovebirds probably need some time alone anyways... By the way, have we met before?"

"I don't think so."

"So why do I feel like I've seen your face before?"

"I hope you swiped right."

"Haha! Funny guy."

"Let's have a look at this curry then. Mmm, this looks delicious! Chickpeas?"

"Yeah, Elsa is kinda vegan."

"I'm a big fan of chickpeas. Big fan."

"I'm glad."

"What about you?"

"Me too."

"No, I mean, are you also kinda vegan?"

"Ah! I see. Well, I'm mostly vegetarian now, although I sometimes eat fish. And I did try going vegan when I first moved in with Elsa two years ago, but I crumbled. I feel like my body just isn't cut out for it."

"Yeah, I've heard it's tough."

"It is. It really is. But hopefully one day I'll try again and succeed. What about you? What do you eat?"

"I eat whatever's closest to me, really."

"Haha!"

"No, seriously. Like, if I'm at the dinner table and the salt shaker is closer to me than the meatloaf, I'm liable to eat the salt until someone passes me the meatloaf."

"Hahaha! You're funny!"

"And what are you keeping in this big bowl? Damn, you made sangria!"

"You don't like sangria?"

"I do."

"So what is it?"

"I feel kinda stupid now."

"Why?"

"Cos we brought sangria too, didn't we."

"Ah, that's fine. No worries."

"Nah, we should've brought something else. Miguel had this special Irish whiskey that he wanted to bring, but I insisted on our national sangria."

"You're Spanish then?"

"Yeah."

"I love Spain."

"Well, I was born there, but I've lived here most of my life. And you're from Norway, right?"

"Yes, although I've also been here for a long time now. Anyway, before we get too distracted, let me get you a knife and a chopping board so you can get started on your sangria."

"Really?"

"Oh, for sure. I feel like when it comes to sangria, the more the merrier!"

"Haha! I like your style."

"And after we can even give the two lovebirds one of each and ask them which one they like best."

"You mean like a blind test?"

"Exactly! Like a blind test."

"Oh, now I really like your style! Okay, I accept your challenge... And what will I get if I win?"

"Ha! What will I get when I win?"

"Anything."

"Anything?"

"Yep, absolutely anything you want—provided I can afford it, of course... And as long as it's, you know, not immoral."

"Haha! Well, I'm very low-maintenance, so I'm sure you'll be able to afford whatever I pick. But I'm also quite adventurous, so I feel like we should probably agree on a definition of moral before I get carried away!"

"Haha! Let me think... Okay, how about this. Anything that you wouldn't be ashamed to search online on a shared computer without deleting your browsing history after."

"Hahaha! Okay, agreed. Then let the games begin and let the best sangria win!"

"Haha! I like that. It rhymes!"

"I know."

"But wait. What will I get if I win?"

"Okay Hugo, let's not stray beyond the realms of possibility..."

* * *

Elsa and Miguel hugged with force then shifted inside the hug until their faces met. The lips contain some of the highest concentrations of Meissner's corpuscles (touch receptors) in the skin. Furthermore, a disproportionally large number of neurones in the primary somatosensory cortex are activated at the touch of the lips. So it's not just a cultural thing.

"I've missed you."

"Have you really?"

"Of course I have. Why do you ask such a silly question?"

"If it's 'of course' and if it's 'such a silly question' then isn't yours also a silly comment?"

"What's got into you? Is it that minty weed you've been smoking?"

"Nothing's gotten into me. Anyway, how have you been? I've hardly got a word out of you since Friday."

"I've been busy."

"Busy with your other guy?"

"Stop. Don't talk like that."

"Relax. I'm joking."

"Well, I don't see you laughing. And you'll certainly never see me laughing at that sort of joke."

"Alright, alright, I won't joke about it again."

"Good."

"What are you two lovebirds bickering over?"

"Nothing."

"Girl, I hope you haven't been taking out your viva stress on him."

"What's a viva?"

"Hasn't she told you? She has to defend her doctoral thesis on Tuesday!"

"No, she didn't tell me!"

"Thanks, Maria."

"Why didn't you want me to know?"

"It's not that I didn't want you to know. It's just that I didn't want to talk about it. I get nervous when I talk about it."

"Girl, I'm going to bring you a drink—you look like you need it. Actually, I'm going to bring you both a drink. Actually no, it's two drinks each!"

"What is she talking about?"

"You should know. She's your flatmate! But, Elsa, I

119

don't like the idea of you not feeling comfortable enough to tell me that sort of stuff."

"Okay lovebirds, here come the drinks! These two cups contain one sangria, and these two glasses contain the other, so take one of each and tell us which one you prefer."

"And I have some sparkling water here to cleanse the palate in between tastings."

"I can tell from the smell which one's Maria's. I recognise the unmistakable ani—"

"Shh! Girl, you'll ruin the test!"

"Oops, sorry!"

"Well, that's no good. If it's not a blind test for you then how can we be sure your opinion is unbiased?"

"It's not like I'm going to pick Maria's over yours simply because she's my friend!"

"Sorry, Elsa. We're gonna have to let Miguel be the sole judge. I don't want any irregularities or Hugo might go back on his word."

"Ooh! What was the wager?"

"He promised me anything I want if I win. Anything! His words, not mine."

"How tempting..."

"Maria, I'll warn you. Be careful what you wish for because Hugo always honours his bets."

"Well I certainly hope so! Anyway, drink and give us your verdict."

"Don't let me down, bro."

"Mmm... Glass is nice. Fruity, but packs a punch."

"Here. Have some sparkling water to cleanse the palate."

"Oh, wow! Okay, cup wins, hands down."

"Haha! Yes, I win. Of course."

"Bro, what the—"

"What?"

"How you gonna do me dirty like that?"

"How can I do you dirty if I didn't even know which was which? But there's just no fucking comparison, bro. The sangria in the cup is miles better."

"Elsa, do you think so too? Do you think hers is miles better than mine?"

"Oh, so now that my sangria has been declared the winner, now you want her non-unbiased opinion?"

"Sorry, Hugo. Yours is nice, although perhaps a bit too strong. But hers is just so perfectly balanced. It has these harmonic layers of flavour which come to you in waves, even after you've swallowed it."

"Yes, I'm getting a wonderful aftertaste also."

"Wonderful, balanced, harmonious... just some of the many accolades that have been lavished on my award-winning sangria."

"What award?"

"Bitch, the my-sangria-tastes-better-than-Hugo's award, for starters!"

"Haha! Okay, fine. And what are you going to ask for your trophy?"

"I don't know yet. I feel like I need to mull it over... Anyway, I'm gonna go check on the rice. It should be ready by now."

"And I'm going toilet to lick my wounds—I mean, wash my hands."

"So I guess it's just us two again."

"I guess so. Show me your room."

"My room? Yeah, sure, come."

"It's very nicely decorated. Is this traditional Scandinavian design?"

"Well, I'd love to say that this was decorated according to a particular style, but truth be told it's just an eclectic mix of whatever I've managed to get my hands on in the three years that I've been in England."

"I like it."

"Thanks."

"Who are these people? Your parents?"

"No, that's Aada and Aku, my siblings."

"Siblings? But they're so old—I mean, no disrespect but, compared to you."

"My dad had them young and had me late."

"How young and how late?"

"Mid-twenties and late forties."

"Wow! All three of you with the same mum?"

"No, my dad Elias had them with Iida, their mother. This is her here. And then they separated, and then he met my mother Aino. Here."

"I see. And do your siblings have any children of their own? Do you have any nieces and nephews your own age?"

"Funnily enough, they always joke about this when we get together for Christmas or whatever. They say they both got enough child-rearing experience for a lifetime bringing me up! They pretty much part-raised me because my parents travelled so much."

"Ah, fair enough. And what's this?"

"That's my cuddly."

"What does that mean?"

"It's something I always cuddle when I sleep. It comforts me."

"Can I touch it?"

"Of course."

"It feels like the bag of a sleeping bag—if you know what I mean."

"Yes, that's exactly what it is! But there's something about that glossy polyester against my face that lulls me into a blissful sleep every time."

"How long have you had it?"

"Since I was a Cadette. So, since I was eleven or twelve."

"You were in the military?"

"No, I was in the Girl Scouts."

"Haha! That's hilarious."

"Why is that hilarious?"

"You're right. It's not. I don't know why I laughed."

"Hahaha! I'm just pulling your leg. Of course it's hilarious! But we've all done something cringe in our youth."

"True."

"Anyway, you should get yourself a cuddly. First you'll need to figure out what yours is, because everybody can have a different item that comforts them. Mine just happens to be this, but yours could be anything. But the good thing is that once you find it, you'll never have nightmares again."

"Is that right?"

"Yes, I guarantee it."

"We'll see."

"Although maybe you don't want to find your cuddly. I remember you telling me that your dreams help you in your creative process..."

"And what about Maria's room?"

"Hers is the door opposite this one."

"Can I see it?"

"Er, maybe we should ask permission first?"

"Never mind. Another time maybe."

"Oh, whatever! I'll just show you. I know for a fact she's got nothing she wishes to hide. Come."

"Wow, look at all this!"

"Yeah, she must have at least one souvenir from each of the countries she's visited. And she's travelled a lot."

"These wooden masks are amazing. You know they— Whoa! What the fuck is that?!"

"That's her dildo collection."

"But I thought you just said..."

"Yes, well, she's not exactly trying to hide them, is she?"

"Clearly not! She's damn near built a shrine for them!"

"Haha!"

"You two lovebirds stop giggling and come to the table. Dinner is ready!"

"Ah, I'm gonna miss her!"

"Miss her?"

"Oh, it's just an expression. Come, let's go eat!"

"So, according to Elsa, no one at this table has any food allergies."

"Yeah, I don't have any of those."

"Me neither."

"Good, because this curry has nuts—almonds."

"Powdered?"

"Yes. Pass me your plate."

"I love powdered almonds. Actually, it's the secret ingredient in my signature chocolate cake."

"I doubt that. How hungry are you?"

"Hahaha! You're quick on the draw."

"I know."

"Haha! And I'm starving."

"Good. Here you go."

"Thanks."

"Miguel, say when..."

"That's enough, thanks. Okay, Maria, that's enough. Maria!"

"I didn't hear you say 'when'. Elsa."

"Haha! She always does this. She's a feeder. You have to start saying 'when' as soon as she hand her the—When! When! When! Gosh, Maria!"

"Alright, no need to shout! I heard you the first time... My turn. I love serving guests first because it means I get the burnt rice, which is my favourite. Mmm, look at all this golden toasted deliciousness. Ah, it's the best! So, everyone got everything they need? Then let's begin."

"Wow! This is just..."

"Holy shit, this is fucking amazing!"

"Oh my god, yes Maria, you've really outdone yourself this time!"

"Mmm... Yes, it came out good. (The tamarind instead of sugar worked.)"

"I think Hugo and I are gonna have to start coming here every Sunday for curry nights."

"Honestly, this is truly the most legit green curry I've had outside of Thailand."

"Aw, thanks! And when did you visit Thailand?"

"I lived there for over a year, about five years ago."

"Five years ago... So that must have been—wait, I was also there in 2012!"

"What a coincidence!"

"Yeah, maybe you guys bumped into each other!"

"Which part were you in?"

"In the north, on the outskirts of Doi Inthanon National Park."

"Shut the fuck up! Maybe that's why your face seems so familiar. I spent a few days trekking Doi Inthanon."

"(I think they're hitting it off!)"

"She thinks we can't hear her—just ignore her. Anyway, did you live there the whole time you were in Thailand or did you move around? And what did you get up to?"

"You're right. Sorry for whispering at the table, guys. And I hope I haven't made you feel uncomfortable, Hugo."

"It's alright, Elsa. I'm not one to stand on ceremony. Well, I was working and living in a resort, of sorts."

"Ah, how lovely!"

"Yeah, the location was incredible, although the whole business was just a cover-up for a safrole operation in the east, in the border with Cambodia."

"Holy shit Hugo, that's so fucking rad!"

"You're really spilling your guts tonight, bro."

"I don't mind. Somehow, I trust these girls."

"Thank you for sharing."

"I don't get it, guys. What's safrole?"

"Sorry, Elsa, I should've explained. Safrole is a natural oil produced from the sap of a rare tree native to Southeast Asia. Among other things, it is used as a precursor in the manufacture of MDMA."

"Oh."

"That's right, Elsa. You're dining with a leading money launderer for an international drug cartel!"

"Don't listen to him, Elsa. I don't launder money anymore. And I was never part of any drug cartel—we were a syndicate."

"Potatoes/potatoes, bro."

"Let's not argue semantics. What was the nature of your role in the organisation, Hugo?"

"Elsa!"

"What?"

"Girl, don't ask him like that."

"Like what?"

"Like you're a fed taking his deposition!"

"It's okay, I don't mind answering her questions... So I was hired as a hotel manager by my uncle. He needed to export safrole to Canada, so he set the whole thing up to look like his Canadian buyers were rich tourists spending lots of dollars in my luxury hotel. But really what I was managing was a barebones hostel at most—and I use the word 'barebones' generously..."

"Well, that doesn't sound too bad. It doesn't sound as if you had to chop off your enemies' heads or anything."

"No, it wasn't bad at all. At first, I just spent my days hiking and reading. And once I got settled in, I got really into the whole mindfulness and meditation thing. It was probably the most relaxing and peaceful time in my life until that point. In fact, I don't think I would be exaggerating if I told you that those Buddhist monks I studied under made me who I am today."

"That's amazing!"

"It is. I'm happy for you."

"Thanks"

"And why did you leave?"

"As these things go, my uncle eventually got caught. Some person he crossed in the past snitched on him, and now he's living his days in a prison cell in British Columbia. And I think the DEA wants to charge him once his

Canadian sentence is served."

"Damn bro, I didn't know that last part."

"It's for the best. That enterprise morally bankrupted him. But, at least from the last few letters we've exchanged, I can tell that he's slowly healing."

"I'm glad to hear it, bro... I'd like to propose a toast. To second chances!"

"And to Maria's amazing curry and award-winning sangria!"

"Well if we're gonna toast to my cooking, then I'd like to toast to Elsa's viva on Tuesday!"

"Oh, don't remind me! Okay, well if everyone else has proposed a toast, then I suppose I should do likewise. To new friendships!"

"Cheers!"

"Cheers!"

"Cheers!"

"Cheers!"

13 THE DOUBLE DATE
(PART 2: PHD)

They sat in a tight circle under garden blankets and a charcoal sky. A mint and weed shisha burned in the centre. And a radial hose dispatched psychic clouds to tractable bronchi. Ten-eighty degrees later, following a unanimous vote (if you exclude her own), Elsa stood up to present her thesis.

"A sustainable pension system in the UK under a protracted low-growth paradigm." She paused. She held on tight as she rode the dizzying crest of a surging wave of THC. It fleeted and landed her intact but disoriented. She looked around; they were looking at her. Hugo, Maria, Miguel—Miguel! A sudden rush of venous blood to the head.

"Let me start from the beginning. A year before I moved to London to start my PhD, I was at my family home in the country. I'd been going through a bit of a rough patch, so I'd gone there to unwind for a few weeks. It's really peaceful out there. I wish I could show it to you. It's in Western Finland, on a little island in an archipelago off the coast. The cabin is sandwiched between the beach and the sea on one side and a pine grove on the other. It's literally the perfect place to unwind.

I remember waking up early one autumn morning— really early, before sunrise. I was feeling euphoric because my doctor had, well, anyway... So I got out of bed and decided to read Atlas Shrugged, the book that Iida had given to me for my eighteenth birthday but I'd never started because I'd always been too intimidated to. I went to the kitchen to make myself a pot of earl grey, and I sat in my dad's armchair drinking it and reading. Who is John Galt? I finished that first chapter and found myself filled with too much kinetic energy to sit still. So I got dressed for the outdoors, grabbed Timon & Pumbaa from their kennels, and disappeared into the fog and darkness.

You may be wondering where I'm going with this. This is the story of how I came to choose my research topic. It all began on that one pivotal day. And I can remember the events of that morning better than yesterday's breakfast.

It is true what they say that it's always darkest before dawn. Running blind that morning was extremely exhilarating. If I hadn't had my two fearless Karelian Bear Dogs running next to me, I might have been afraid—but as it was, I felt free. And my feet had an unnatural lightness to them. I noticed the first twilight staining the darkness, and each brighter step filled us with confidence and carried us further away from the house and the shore. We followed the creeping fog up a steep hill and beat the sunrise to the top. Suddenly the fog that had surrounded us abandoned us, leaving in its stead the black treetops and a pale red band and the receding indigo. And I collapsed to my knees from exhaustion at the foot of a pinnacling pine tree.

It was as if all my tiredness condensed inside me. I sat on my heels and attempted to catch my breath, but I started hyperventilating instead. Then the three of us were exhaling loud clouds, but their throat didn't hurt like mine, and they didn't have a sharp pain in their chest like I. I felt like crying. All my strength had deserted me, and suddenly

I felt insignificant and forgettable. Although that's probably misleading because I didn't feel in the sense of being aware of my emotions. No, I simply experienced. And it was only in retrospect that I was able to interpret those experiences."

She looked up. The charcoal sky was brimming with scattered sounds from all over London. She closed her eyes and touched it with her face, and smelled it as it entered her nostrils, and tasted it as it exited her mouth.[10]

"The chest pain kept stabbing me and draining me of my willpower. I was shutting down. Life and death seemed strangely compatible. There was an opaque energy inside me, and in a misguided survival attempt I closed my eyes and tried to find it. But then the strangest thing happened. You know how thoughts are normally processed in the first person? The implicit 'I think' that precedes all verbal thought. And you know how thoughts are normally followed by an emotional or even physical reaction to their perceived significance? Well, this thought was different. This thought—if I can even call it that—was spoken not in the first person and not in my inner voice, and its repercussions extended far beyond the physiological because I was overwhelmed with a rush of energy of a kind I couldn't even recognise, let alone process:

'The truth isn't within. It's out there!'

I opened my eyes to try to contain this vertigo, but the sky enveloped me with a force so fierce I feared I might drown in it—or burn in it, since the atmosphere was on fire

---

[10] The heavens look far, unreachable, but in reality they envelop us and nurture us. Unfortunately, most of us take that for granted—until it's too late.

now and the clouds had the hue of molten metal. You see, we had crossed that irreversible inflexion point of the twilight, and I felt as if I was crossing an inflexion point in my life—escorted by two fearless Anubis.

And just then, the first ray shone through the horizon. It tapped me with powerful momentum, with a physical mass. And I felt it. And it triggered something, a chain reaction. And suddenly, it all rushed in. Everything that had ever been, rushed in. Every truth, far outstripping every fact that I'd ever known to be true, rushed in. It was all around me. I couldn't escape it: God, Allah, The Tao, Mother Nature, Time, whatever your tribe calls it! I was shown a beautiful completeness in our existence that I had never appreciated before. And I realised then for the first time that life and death are not incompatible, that they're inseparable parts of the same unit: the endless cycle of energy. And I grasped its universality and stopped fearing for my particular life or death. In short, I found peace."

She closed her eyes to recall that sensation... And she felt it again.

"I had been humbled—in the most positive sense of the word. I was infinitesimally small but an inseparable part of All. I felt powerful, eternal, with the strength of the universe on my side. And my two dogs, they were looking at me, guarding me, protecting me with their undying loyalty. And the pine trees, they were watching over me, sheltering me, forever ready to sacrifice their flesh for my warmth. And the sun and the sky too, they were as parents to a child, the source of all my energy, and the guiding light beyond all unanswerable questions. And I belonged to all of them. My fauna, my flora, my heavens: I was made to serve them."

She paused, grabbed the pipe, inhaled, exhaled...

White smoke rises and dissipates into the ether.

"I guess you could say I had the textbook religious experience. Anyway, that was the moment I decided I wouldn't be going back to work as a management consultant. (So you know, Hugo, that's what I'd been doing since finishing my masters: advising large corporates on demographic economics—their future consumers, their pension liabilities, that sort of thing...) So, I emailed my boss my resignation the morning after and, over the following weeks, went about devising a plan for my future. I wanted to choose a path that was conscious, holistic, and that would allow me to express what I'd been shown on that hill. I wanted to live faithfully by the spirit of that experience. I wanted to find my way to serve the world.

Before that day and as far back as I can faithfully remember, I regarded my happiness as insufficient and superficial, but I didn't quite know why. But on that day, I understood that it was because even though my physical and psychological needs were being met, I still lacked purpose and meaning in my life. And after that day, I started noticing that many of the people around me were faced with a similar problem.

Then a thought struck me. Maybe not all of us will ever fulfil our potentialities, but for sure all of us will never fulfil them independently. And over time but under scrutiny that thought hardened into a conviction. That the spiritual development of the average individual can be no deeper than what its cultural environment will allow. That for people to be fulfilled, there needs to be a social structure that respects and promotes spirituality. And what is our social structure now? What is the one thread connecting all people all over the world? Capital! Capitalism is the one supreme religion, the only universal faith.

So that's how I narrowed down my university department. Now, don't get me wrong. I'm not trying to claim that it's only through economics that the world can be changed. In fact, one could easily argue that we are on the cusp of far more revolutionary advances in nuclear fusion, molecular biology, and artificial intelligence. But frankly, it would've been near impossible for me to do a PhD in those disciplines given my academic background and professional experience. And most of all, it wasn't at all clear to me that advances in those disciplines would be in the aggregate positive for humanity. I wanted to contribute to a social revolution for the betterment of all— an emancipation of the human race into a higher plane of existence. In practical terms, I wanted to help progress the current economic structure governing the productive forces of society."

She took a sip from her cup. That anise sangria was something special. Maria was a goddess.

"After I had settled on Economics, I started trying to find a specific topic. And during the preliminary phase of this unimaginably long and arduous task, I found that the handful of people who genuinely shared my concerns could be split into two camps: radical anarchists living in permaculture communities dotted all over the temperate regions of the free world, and radical scholars in the novel field of Ecological Economics. I chose the latter, and they opened my eyes to something truly novel and exciting. Ecological economists emphasise the need to regard the economy as subservient to society, which in turn is delimited by our finite ecosystem. They shun the universal pursuit of economic growth and advocate a de-growth towards a steady-state economy—that is, a socially sustainable economy whose scale falls within planetary boundaries. It's not that they're blind to the historical benefits of economic growth, nor do they deny the positive correlation between happiness and income up to a certain level, but they insist that the marginal benefits to humans of income growth decrease past a certain point while its damages to the environment carry on increasing monotonically, and sometimes even non-linearly once certain thresholds are breached.

'Exponential growth in a finite domain is unsustainable.'

This fundamental idea was so simple that I almost rejected it at first. I thought there must have been a reason why it hadn't caught on already. And of course there's a reason. The reason is all around us. We humans are consumed by a need for growth! But where did this growth fetish come from? Well, there is no definitive answer to any question worth asking—as a wise man once said... However, I did manage to piece together my own theory from disparate texts on behavioural psychology, anthropology, and evolutionary biology. To summarise, I believe our growth fetish to be an artefact of our imperfect awakening from unconsciousness, of our banishment from the Garden of Eden. But irrespective of its origin, once I accepted this human condition for what it is, it became startlingly obvious to me that the preservation of our ecosystem is the single most significant issue that our civilisation, no, that our planet has faced since it entered the Anthropocene. And I became convinced of the need to reach a steady-state economy without delay.

Once I found my topic, I started drafting my research

proposal. I was trying to come up with a question that hadn't been asked before—or at least find one that hadn't been answered yet. I began with the big unanswered questions: What are the viable alternatives to the current economic regime? How much would they help us achieve social and ecological sustainability? How costly would it be to implement them? Etcetera, etcetera... But after speaking to a few potential supervisors, I very quickly realised, or rather was made to realise, that I was overreaching. And so I moved on to the smaller unasked questions. And I decided to make my life easier by drawing on my strengths and experiences—namely, demographic economics. Eventually I found my supervisor, and together we settled on the super exciting topic of pensions because a well-functioning pension system is fundamental to achieving social sustainability under any economic regime.

Actually, in an ideal world I would have liked to research Universal Basic Income. But I wasn't able to find any funding for that topic—no scholarships, no government grants, no industrial sponsorships, nothing. So my supervisor wily suggested that I realign my research to pensions and, lo and behold, the big funds came knocking. It's silly because, when you think about it, UBI is really just a special case of a public pension system with the eligibility age lowered all the way down to 18 or 16 or whatever.

But anyway, sexy pensions. High-income countries are facing structural funding shortfalls because of ageing populations and plateauing productivity rates. I've outlined these pension deficits and their structural causes in the introduction of my thesis, and I've also perfunctorily performed the mandatory literature review. In the main body, I've modelled and analysed the effect that alternative economic paradigms might have on the affordability of the UK's public pension system and on the viability of its private pension industry. And I've done a pretty decent job of it—if I may say so myself—because I've provided fund managers and policymakers with what I believe to be rather accurate estimates of private and public pension funding deficits in a perennially low-growth or steady-state economy. In the conclusion, I've offered some possible solutions for closing those deficits. And not just from classical economics, my solutions were very much inspired by anthropological studies of current alternative communities and—don't laugh—by imagined civilisations depicted in science fiction. Lastly, as an avenue for further research—and this is something that I'm particularly proud of—I've given away two ready-made PhD proposals along with literature reviews and links to potential funding sources. I've done this so as to encourage budding economists to join the ecological revolution! Or not just economists really, but any bright and determined minds. In fact, academic researchers alone will never be able to herald the kind of societal change our planet needs, and there are many thought experiments that would be better executed and publicised by writers, artists, and others of that ilk."

She paused and waited for an acknowledgement that didn't come.

"That's it, really. That's my PhD—in a nutshell. Inside the shell of a very large and rather long-winded nut..."

It still didn't come.

"I hope my research helps the world. I really do. But even if it doesn't, even if these past three years have been no more than a self-indulgent exercise in intellectual masturbation, even if my thesis reads as no more than the excrements of an unquiet mind, even if my peers tear it apart for some unforgivable flaw in my analysis, or even if somehow the exact same research has already been carried out by another researcher that neither my supervisor nor I knew about, even if, if, if, I don't regret it, because I've gained so many positive things from the process. Aside from the knowledge and self-discipline I've acquired, aside from the way I've become so acquainted and comfortable with the limits of my intelligence, aside from the serenity I've had to embrace in order to endure the seemingly never-ending tests of patience, aside from, from, from, I have found a love and respect for myself that I had been missing for a long time but that I now realise is an indispensable ingredient of contentment. And I've passively learnt a new language, one that allows me to interpret my emotional energy, and communicate with my soul. And with this language I'm also better able to feel the world around me with more clarity, appreciating all that is beautiful and not fearing all that seems cruel. Like that time with my dogs atop the soaring hill under the firelight bloom of the rising sun... Life!"

She paused again and waited for an acknowledgement that seemed as if it would never come.

"Jesus Christ, Hugo! What the fuck was in that weed?!"

"Don't even try and shift the blame on me. That must have been your award-winning sangria!"

"Elsa, I say this without any reservations: you have the most beautiful mind of any person I have ever met!"

"Guys, don't move. I want to capture this moment. I'm going to get my selfie drone!"

14 THE DOUBLE DATE
(PART 3: SEX)

While Elsa was teaching Miguel the basics of drone flying, Maria asked Hugo to help her carry the hookah and the empty sangria bucket and cups back into the house. And as soon as they put the stuff down on the kitchen counter, she started making out with him.

"What was that for?"

"Is there a problem?"

"No, ma'am. No problem. I just wasn't expecting it."

"Tomorrow we'll say it was the minty weed and the anise sangria, but right now I just feel like being close to you, and I don't want to overthink it."

And she kissed him again, with more pressure this time. Their nasal breathing grew louder as their tongues twisted and their bodies pressed against each other. She put one hand underneath his shirt and rubbed his lower back. This sent a chill up his spine that clenched his jaw and bit her bottom lip. She gasped. He picked her up, placed her on the kitchen counter, pulled her head back, and ran his tongue from her clavicle to her earlobe. A soft moan slipped out of her mouth and made its way into his ear. She stopped him.

"What's wrong?"

"What's your postcode?"

"My postcode?"

"Yes, I wanna call an Uber."

"Oh shit! You wanna come back to mine?"

"Yes, why, don't you want me to?"

"No, I mean, yes, I want you to!"

"So invite me then. Invite me!"

"Alright. (Ahem!) Milady, would you like to spend the night at mine? I have a very comfortable couch for you. Haha!"

"You idiot!"

"Here, I'll just order it from my phone... If I can find the bloody thing!"

"Isn't it in your pocket?"

"Nah, what you felt was my burner."

"Nah, what I felt was your boner!"

"Haha! Touché."

"Never mind, just give me the postcode. I'll order it."

"Okay, it's W9 2AE."

"Alright, ordered. Now go find your pay-monthly phone so we can get out of here."

"Wait, I wanna go toilet first."

"Okay but hurry up cos I need to go too."

"Oh, ladies first then."

"What a gentleman. Knock, knock."

"What?"

"Knock, Knock! C'mon, you know this one!"

"Oh, yeah, sure, who's there?"

"Hugo."

"Hugo who?"

"Hu-go first! Hahaha!"

"Oh no, you didn't!"

"Go! Go! Go!"

"Alright, alright, I'm going!"

Elsa was teaching Miguel complex drone manoeuvres when Maria and Hugo came back, this time with their jackets on.

"Maria! Where are you taking him?"

"We're just going to the corner shop to get some Gummy Bears."

"Yeah, you guys want anything?"

"Bro, can you get me some of that Ben & Jerry's Chocolate Fudge Brownie ice cream? Oh, and try get the non-dairy version if they have it."

"Can you WhatsApp me it? Cos I might not remember it otherwise."

Maria prodded Hugo out of the front garden.

"Why did you ask them if they wanted anything from the corner shop?"

"To make it more believable."

"You do realise we're not going back, right?"

She had a point.

After one last drone manoeuvre, her pièce de résistance, Miguel helped Elsa tidy up the garden chairs and blankets.

"They're taking really long."

"They're not coming back."

"What? How do you know?"

"Because she said Gummy Bears, and because she just messaged me."

"Oh, so where did they go?"

"They went, and I quote: 'back to his to fuck his brains out!'"

"Oh, wow! Well, lucky for him, I guess."

"Lucky for you! Because we now have the flat all to

ourselves... Come." They went inside; she led him by the hand to the living room couch.

"Hey, so what made you reply to me?"

"What do you mean?"

"My DM. I didn't think you'd reply. Well, definitely not so soon, anyway. To be honest, I wasn't even sure I'd be your type."

"Well, if you're fishing for compliments, I'll give you one: you're probably most women's type. And as for replying so soon: you were the first person to write to me."

"What?"

"You were the first person to write to me."

"No, I heard you. But I don't buy that for one second!"

"It's true! I'd never had a stranger message me on Instagram before, and quite frankly I didn't know what the protocol was, but for some reason I thought it would be rude not to reply."

"How is that even possible?"

"My account had always been private, and my previous profile pic of an emaciated polar bear stranded on a tiny iceberg in the middle of an ocean was not exactly dick bait."

"Haha! True. So what made you change your profile to public?"

"Maria. Maria made me change it. Maria's many, many months of incessant badgering made me change it."

"I see."

"But I'm glad she did. Although I'm thinking of changing it back to private."

"Why?"

"Why am I glad or why am I thinking of changing it back?"

"I don't know, both? Never mind. Shit, I think I'm

fucking high!"

"You want a glass of water?"

"No, I'm just waiting for that Ben & Jerry's that Hugo's gonna—ah, fuck!"

"Here, I'm going to make us both a nice, revitalising pot of green tea."

"Yeah, that's probably a good idea. Thanks."

"Just hold on. Don't fall asleep on me!"

Elsa came back with one full teapot and two empty cups.

"Careful, it's hot!"

"Mmm, smells delicious! What is it?"

"I've mixed some green tea with some chamomile and some fennel."

"Amazing."

"Hey, Miguel, do you realise it's been three weeks since we met?"

"Yes, I do. Exactly three weeks to the day."

"Are you feeling better now?"

"Yes. That tea was amazing. Thank you."

"Good, and I'm glad you liked it. So, Miguel, did you bring condoms with you?"

"What? I mean, yes!"

"Good. Then go to my bedroom and wait for me there."

"Yes, ma'am!"

"And connect your phone to my speaker and play some music."

"Slow jams?"

"Hmm... No, actually. Pearl Jam, Ten."

This page has been left blank intentionally.

Miguel's ejaculation (through a hitherto unknown torn condom) at the same time as Elsa's internal orgasm wasn't the climax—what followed was. From their lotus position, she uncrossed her legs behind him, and with his still-erect penis and catalytic semen inside her, guided him back with a vertiginous kiss. And there they stayed, prone and supine, for an eternal moment... She embraced him with her vagina, legs, feet, torso, arms, hands, fingers, neck, hair, weight, warmth, breath, pulse, affection, validation, acceptance. Then, two precise palpebral kisses perforated the last layer separating the two, the two aspects of his personality, the two aspects of every human's personality: the masculine and the feminine. Suddenly he shed a tear; she tasted it before he noticed it. And then another; she swallowed it before his eyes. Next, a hydraulic cacophony of viral visions and jousting energies fracked through his puncta. And for the first time in almost nine years, Miguel cried. And cried. And cried. This was the climax, incomparable to any before or since. Elsa knew without asking that talking wouldn't have helped. All she could do was take him in, take him in entirely, take all his self, all his other selves, his previous selves, his future selves, all of them as different perspectives of the same person, of the same entity, take them all in as one. And she did. She did. With one heartfelt prayer, she took all of Miguel in. And he drowned to sleep to the white sound of her fingertips against his shaved head, like shimmering water rippling above on the surface. Release.

Miguel was standing naked in the middle of a secluded pond at the bottom of a tropical waterfall, and Elsa was swimming naked under the surface towards his penis which was an electric eel, when the hoarse friction of her vintage wooden chest of drawers woke him up. Now he had the rare luxury of seeing her get dressed in the morning. Peach cotton knickers rising gracefully under a mauve cotton towel...

She was sorry to break the bad news to him when she noticed he was awake and ogling her, but he had slept through the main attraction: her naked morning yoga. Imagine Elsa, naked, doing yoga, naked.

There was once a superstitious man who played the National Lottery with the same lucky numbers every week for decades. Then one day, just as he was about to pay for his ticket, he remembered that it was his umpteenth wedding anniversary and decided to use his last pound to buy his wife a pretty card instead. No prizes for guessing what happened next. But the point is, whatever the name of the indescribable countenance that this superstitious man must have carried throughout that day, Miguel now carried it too.

"Anyway, Miguel, what do you like to eat for breakfast? I was thinking of making some avocado toast and a smoothie."

"Some what toast?"

"Ha! You heard me!"

"Great... Well, I suppose I should get up and help you."

"Oh, no, that's not necessary. You relax, and I'll call you when it's ready."

"No, no. Better to face the music."

There is something uniquely familial about cooking together, especially breakfast. It had been a while since either of them had done this, so they both entered the kitchen understandably tense. But their nerves quickly evaporated into a comforting sense of excitement once they got started. They worked elegantly, styling out accidental collisions with caresses and kisses so that their coming together looked intentional, if not choreographed. Elsa blended a very simple yet effective smoothie with three bananas, 250g of frozen blueberries, and 500ml of almond milk. She topped it with linseeds and poppy seeds. Miguel semi-spread one and a half perfectly ripe avocado onto three slices of sourdough rye bread. He seasoned it with lime, chilli, salt and—

"I think the black pepper in this grinder has run out."

"Oh, well, there should be a refill packet in that corner cupboard."

"Aha! Found it."

"And there's some scissors in that top drawer if you need them."

"It's alright. I'll manage."

But he didn't manage. He burst the little plastic bag open, sending 280 black peppercorns flying in all directions. Most of them landed on the floor, some landed on the kitchen counter, and one even landed, impressively, inside the pepper mill. But he was not impressed; that lone dutiful peppercorn was of no consolation to him. He stood frozen for a beat, two, three, furiously silent. It's as if he became, at that point in space and time, the personification of self-loathing. Elsa had never seen him so angry.

"Hey... Hey, Miguel, it's alright... It's no big deal."

He burst through his silence: "Fuck! How could I've been so fucking stupid?!"

"Hey, don't beat yourself up over some spilt peppercorns."

147

15 THE JOB OFFER

"Hi Elsa, I hope you're okay. I just called because there's something I want to say."

"Hi! Sorry for late reply. What did you want to say?"

"I wanted to apologise for losing it in your kitchen like that yesterday. It was completely out of order and I hope I didn't scare you."

"It's fine, no worries."

"What are you up to tonight? These two have been holed up in their room for hours!"

"I'm preparing tonight and all day tomorrow. I've got my viva in ~36h!"

"Yes, of course. I'll let you get on with it then. Good luck! Xx"

"Thanks, good night. Xx"

"Oh one last thing…"

"Shoot."

"I feel a bit awkward asking especially over WhatsApp."

"What is it?"

"Did you take an emergency contraceptive today?"

"Yes I did."

"Okay that's good to know!"

"Don't worry I'm not trying to get pregnant. Lol"

* * *

"Elsa?"

"Maria? Is that really you?"

"Hey, how's things?"

"I thought I'd never see you again!"

"Shut up, silly. I've only been gone two nights."

"How was Hugo the Buddhist drug dealer?"

"I really like him. He's so adorable."

"Yeah, he actually is. And you look happy."

"Well, let me tell you: the sex, it was so good..."

"Yeah?"

"Yes, amazing! We were so connected. I wanted to consume every part of him, and I could tell that he wanted to do more or less the same to me. And okay, he's a little bit shy but, I'll get him there."

"Oh boy, I hope you didn't scare him."

"Nah, I'm going easy on him—for now."

"Good idea."

"And he likes to cuddle after, which I normally hate, but with him it was different. I think it's his smell. It's really comforting, almost familiar."

"His smell?"

"Yeah, he smells like morning wind on the beach."

"Right. Well, as long as you're happy."

"Anyway, enough about me. Tell me, tell me, how was Miguel? You guys finally had sex or what?"

"Yes, we did, finally."

"And? What was it like?"

"It was fine."

"Ooh... That bad?"

"No, it wasn't bad at all!"

"So?"

"I don't know..."

"You don't know? Elsa, this is your first boyfriend since, well, since I've known you! And all you can say is 'it was fine'?"

"He's not my boyfriend."

"Jesus Christ, it's like getting blood from a stone!"

"What do you want me to say?"

149

"Tell me what he said to turn you on, describe how you felt when he undressed you, how he touched you, how many times you climaxed... Tell me everything!"

"He didn't say anything in particular to turn me on after you guys left, but the sexual attraction had been accumulating over the past few weeks. And I undressed myself. And how did he touch me? He touched me like... like he knew what he was doing, basically. I'm guessing he must've had a lot of experience."

"Did he make you come?"

"Yes."

"How many times?"

"Maria, I don't feel like getting into the specifics of my orgasms."

"Orgasms? Plural? So it was more than once!"

Elsa rolled her eyes.

"Alright, fine. Does he have a nice body?"

"You know he does. You've seen his Instagram."

"Yeah, but those abs could've been Photoshopped."

"It's not Photoshop. Flattering lighting, maybe. But he really does have abs—which is sort of baffling to me because he doesn't work out or watch what he eats at all."

"Must be genetic then."

"I guess."

"So..."

"So?"

"Does he have a big dick?"

"Okay, I'm going to my room now."

"Okay, okay, fine! I won't ask you any more questions about the sex. But tell me this: did you tell him you were moving to Sweden?"

"Moving to Sweden?"

"Possibly moving to Sweden. Thinking about moving to Sweden."

"They haven't even offered me a job yet. And even if they did, I haven't yet made up my mind as to whether I'd take it."

"You need to tell him because I might have let it slip yesterday to Hugo that you were moving."

"What? Why?"

"It was an accident. But don't worry, I bought you some time. I made him promise not to tell Miguel."

"Oh yeah, like he's going to withhold information from his boy just to keep a promise to a girl who he's known for one night."

"Oi!"

"Sorry, two nights."

"You can be so nice sometimes."

"I'm just stating facts. Anyway, it doesn't matter. I don't mind if Hugo tells him."

"You don't think Miguel will be upset if Hugo tells him you're moving to Sweden?"

"I don't know how he'll feel, but I do know that his feelings towards my possibly moving to another country are not my responsibility."

"Yeah okay, sure, but I mean, it's not the same you telling him as him finding out from somebody else."

"It's not the same but it's not necessarily any better. For example, it's quite likely that he'll assume his opinion to be a factor in my decision-making process if I tell him personally. And more generally, if an upcoming event is undesirable but inevitable, then prior knowledge of it is hardly ever beneficial."

* * *

"Hey bro, what's up?"

"Hey, what's up, bro? You alone?"

"What do you mean?"

"I mean is Maria-your-future-baby-mama still in the house?"

"Funny. But no, she went home a little while ago."

"Oh, so she's not moving in with us then?"

"Shut up, fool! But why, though? Does she bother you? I thought you liked her."

"Relax. I'm joking. Of course I like her. And I don't mind her being here at all."

"Okay, cool. But let me know if it ever bothers you, though."

"I can do you one better. I can tell you now when it should start to bother you."

"Bother me?"

"Watch out for the first time she does the dishes."

"The dishes?"

"That's how it always starts, bro—with the dishes."

"What you on about?"

"I'm not talking about you cooking for a girl and her doing the dishes after—that would be fair and reasonable, even desirable. I'm talking about when she comes over and straight away starts cleaning a pile of dirty dishes that she had nothing to do with. That's always the first sign a girl's trying to move in with you, so make sure you dump her as soon as it happens."

"Bro, you are proper paranoid. And I'm not dumping Maria, or any chick, just because she likes to clean."

"You don't get it. Nobody likes to clean other people's homes. But you've been warned, my friend."

"Whatever. Anyway, I've been meaning to ask, but I

didn't wanna do it while Maria was around, how was Elsa?"

"Bro, you wouldn't believe it, and I wouldn't be able to explain it. She's just... incredible."

"Was she filthy?"

Miguel kissed his teeth.

"What? Don't tell me she was a starfish!"

"Don't ask me about her like that."

"Why not? You always tell me everything about the girls you fuck. Shit, you've even shown me some of your—what did you use to call it, Erotic Reportage? Haha! You do take good pictures, though. I'll give you that."

"Yeah, well, she's not like the rest of them, so I'm not gonna disrespect her."

"Aha! He finally admits that he disrespects women. I'm proud of you, bro. Acknowledgement is the first step towards growth."

"Fuck you."

"Oh, by the way bro, I gotta tell you something but you absolutely cannot tell Elsa, cos Maria made me promise not to tell you."

* * *

"Hi Elsa, you're probably busy with last-minute preparations for tomorrow. I just wanted to say best of luck with your viva even though I don't think you need it because I'm sure you'll do just fine. Message me after if you want to meet."

"If by last-minute preparations you mean feeling like puking the food that I've been physically unable to eat in the past two days then you're right on the money. And I can message you after, but I won't be able to meet until much later, if at all, because Maria has a whole day planned out for us."

* * *

"Hey how was it? I hope it went well!"

"Yay! I passed!"

"Congratulations! I knew you would. Let me know when you finish with Maria."

"Okay. We're on our way to some super fancy spa she's booked. And she says she's got another surprise for me after. She won't admit it but I'm pretty sure it's The Book of Mormon. I hope so anyway!"

"Okay well maybe tomorrow then?"

"Yeah, I suppose we can meet tomorrow. It'd have to be in the morning though."

"Morning?"

"Yeah, I'm flying to Stockholm in the evening."

"Oh, I didn't know. You never told me."

"Well, it's just for the weekend."

"Okay well I can't do tomorrow morning, so should we schedule something now for when you're back?"

"I'm back Sunday afternoon. You and Hugo fancy having a double date like last week?"

"Sure thing. Let's make it happen."

"Btw, Maria says your house this time. And that it's you boys' turn to cook. Haha!"

"Er, I hope you girls got full-cover medical insurance!"

"LMAO"

* * *

"I know I'm early but damn, where the hell is my Maria and your Hugo? They're not playing that game again, are they?"

"Nah, they just popped out to the store—to get some Gummy Bears."

"Oh boy..."

"Hahaha! Nah, I'm joking. They went to get some missing ingredients for tonight's dinner: roasted vegetable pasta bake."

"Ooh, sounds delicious!"

"And as long as I stay well clear of the kitchen, it will be."

"Haha!"

"Anyway, how was the flight?"

"Fine. Well, you know, apart from the usual pains with security checks, and passport controls, and delays, and queues, and overcrowded overhead compartments, and crying babies on the plane, and—"

"Okay, I get it! Haha! And how was Stockholm?"

"Stockholm was nice. It was starting to get a bit cold already, but at least the skies were clear and sunny."

"It's been getting colder here too—minus the clear and sunny skies."

"I heard."

"So did you get up to anything interesting while you were out there?"

"Well, I had a meeting with some fellow ecological economists on Friday, and then I spent the rest of the weekend catching up with an old friend who's just had her first baby."

"Oh, well congrats to your friend on her first baby."

"He's so cute, so frigging cute. But it's strange because this is the one friend who I never expected to get married and have babies."

"People can change and surprise us."

"Clearly."

"And the meeting? What was it about?"

"Well, to be specific, it was a job interview."

"I see. And did it go well?"

"Yeah."

"So I guess now it's that awkward wait until you hear back from them?"

"Actually they made me an offer on the spot."

"Oh, wow, congratulations. And did you accept their

offer?"

"I told them I would think about it and tell them by Monday."

"Monday is tomorrow."

"Yup."

"So have you decided already?"

"Yes, I'm going to take it. I would be crazy not to. It's the Stockholm Resilience Centre. I'll be researching exactly what I'm interested in alongside some of the most formidable minds in the field."

"That's great news. And the job is presumably there, or do they have offices elsewhere?"

"No, they don't have offices anywhere else. They have people they collaborate with worldwide, but yeah, the job would require me to relocate to Stockholm."

"Well, congratulations. I propose a toast to you moving to Sweden and starting a new chapter in your life. I think this calls for The Quiet Man."

"Yes, finally! I've been dying to taste it."

"Let me go and get it from my room then. Just out of curiosity, when would you start?"

"They were quite flexible on that. They said I could pick my start date."

That Sunday night the pasta was delicious and the whiskey, perfect. But the news had left a bad taste in Miguel's mouth. Still, he did his best to keep up appearances.

"You want me to go back to yours tonight?"

"No, not really."

Miguel was taken aback by Elsa's blunt answer.

"Sorry."

"No, no, don't apologise. But, is everything okay?"

"Yeah, just, you know..."

"What? Oh, that time of the month?"

"No, it's not that."

"Then?"

"I just don't want my thought process to get distracted."

"Thought process?"

"Yeah."

"Listen, I would never want you to pass on an opportunity like this for me or because of me."

"I know that. And I wouldn't. But I just don't want to add any more bitterness to this already bittersweet situation. I'm already quite sad about leaving Maria and London. I don't want to get attached to you too."

"Okay, I get it. I won't ask again."

Elsa was made comfortable by his understanding.

"And tonight I'll just stay here listening to those two wild animals having crazy sex all night."

"Haha! Have you heard them?"

"Have I heard them? Has anyone on this block not heard them? That's the question!"

"Haha! Yeah, she can get quite loud sometimes. No! I meant, er..."

"Haha!"

"Shit! Oh my god, please don't tell her I said that!"

"I won't."

"Or him!"

"Nah, I'm glad Hugo's happy. I wouldn't want to get in the way of that."

"Thanks! And yeah, I'm also glad that they're getting along... So, what do you think? Is it even worth the two flights of stairs to their room to try to say goodbye?"

"Save it. If they've gone back to that game, which they

most probably have, then I doubt they'll even hear you. And even if they do hear you, I doubt they'd ever pause their game for you. Haha!"

"They're so addicted. What is it about anyway?"

"He said it was a—and let's see if I can get this right—a 'multiplayer online survival horror'. Whatever that means."

"You know, it's strange, but I've never known her to be a gamer... Right, well, if and when they finally emerge from their virtual apocalypse, please give them my regards."

"Will do. Wait, how you getting home?"

"Er, I think I'll walk. Probably a good idea to walk off this Quiet Man before I get into bed. By the way, Miguel, you sir have impeccable taste in whiskey!"

"Why thank you, ma'am! I'm glad you liked it. And would you do me the honour of letting me walk you home?"

"No, don't be silly."

"It's not silly. I don't want you walking alone on the Harrow Road this late."

"But if you walk me you'll be faced with having to walk back alone, and it'll be even later by then, so I'll feel obliged to walk you back, and then we'll be back at square one."

"Now who's the one being silly?"

"Fine, okay, this is what we'll do. I will do you the honour of letting you walk me to the bus stop, and from there I'll ride the night bus home."

"Deal."

* * *

"Hello, Miguel."

"Hi, Elsa. I thought you weren't going to pick up!"

158

"No, it's just that my phone was in my other room and I almost didn't hear it."

"Ah, okay. Anyway, how are you?"

"I'm good. I'm really good."

"So have you signed on the dotted line yet?"

"Yes! Well, figuratively speaking, yes. I sent the email this morning, and the director called me straight away to tell me how delighted they all are that I'll be joining them. You know, it actually made me feel quite proud of myself."

"That's nice of them. So what are you doing for the rest of the day?"

"I want to go visit my supervisor and share the good news and maybe take her out for a drink."

"That's nice of you."

"We've grown quite close over the years."

"You know, I dreamt about you last night."

"Oh yeah?"

"Yes. And I think this new job is definitely a good move for you."

"Aw, thanks. I think so too."

"I'm going to miss you, though."

"I'm going to miss you too."

"So what now?"

"What do you mean?"

"Nothing. Hey, did you settle on a start date?"

"Yes, I told them I could start as early as the first of November."

"What?"

"The first of November."

"No, I heard you. But that's in like, two weeks. Why so soon?"

"Well, I'm done with my PhD now, so I thought I might

as well start sooner rather than later."

"But don't you have to look for a place in Stockholm first?"

"Actually, my friend—you know the one that's just had a baby—said I could stay with them until I find a place."

"And what about your room in London? Aren't you gonna lose money by leaving before your notice period?"

"Well no, because I'm going to be earning as soon as I start working. And my friend refuses to accept any rent money. So actually, the sooner I move, the more money I save overall."

"I guess you've got it all figured out then. So what are your plans until you leave?"

"I want to take a relaxing holiday somewhere sunny. This summer has been completely spent indoors finalising my thesis, and soon it will get very dark and cold in Stockholm."

"Maybe we could go on a beach holiday for a few days? Have you ever been to the Canary Islands?"

"Actually, I was thinking of going to Dubai to visit my friend Enia who lives there now."

"What, all-you-can-eat lobster girl?"

"Haha! Yes, exactly!"

"Oh, well, I hear they serve lots of seafood in Dubai, so I'm sure you guys will enjoy it."

"Hahaha! Actually, I'm trying to drag her to the Maldives from there. Direct lights from the Emirates are not expensive and they don't even require a pre-arrival visa."

"Wow, Maldives, that's literally paradise."

"Yes, that's what I've heard. And it's meant to be absolutely perfect for diving. Hopefully, if I'm really lucky,

I might even get to swim with manta rays!"

"Oh, so you guys gonna go diving together?"

"I'm working on it. To be honest, it'll be a miracle if I manage to convince her to scuba dive—I know she shudders at the thought of coming face-to-face with a big fish—but I'm hoping she'll at least agree to come to the Maldives with me."

"Well, if she doesn't go with you, let me know, and maybe I can join you there."

"Hmm... I'm not sure that's a good idea."

"Okay, Elsa, what's going on? I've been trying to ignore the awkwardness, but that's impossible now. You have to explain to me what's changed because I'm struggling to understand you."

"Just yesterday you said that you understood. So why are you pressuring me again?"

"Pressuring you? That's the last thing I'm tryna do. Look, I understand that you're afraid of goodbyes. That's why I'm trying to show you that it doesn't need to be goodbye."

"If me being afraid of goodbyes is what you understood when I told you I didn't want you to come back to mine last night, then I'm sorry I wasn't clearer. What I meant and what I mean is that I don't think it's a good idea to invest any more time and energy into this."

"Elsa."

"What?"

"Why are you being like this?"

"Like what?"

"So cold."

"Look, what do you expect from me?"

"We don't have to stop what we've been building just

because you're moving abroad."

"So what are you saying?"

"I'm saying we could make it work."

"Make what work? You want to have a long-distance relationship, is that what you're proposing?"

"We don't necessarily have to label it a long-distance relationship, but we could at least try to have something."

"Honestly, Miguel, even if you knew what you wanted—and even if I wanted the same—I don't think you'd be capable of providing it."

"I don't like being written off like that. I don't like it one bit."

"Please don't make the next steps any harder than they need to be."

"But the next steps aren't set in stone—that's what I'm trying to show you."

"I'm sorry, Miguel, but I just don't see a future between us."

"You don't see it, or you don't want it?"

"It makes no difference—the outcome is still the same."

"It makes a huge difference to me."

"Look, I don't want to argue about this anymore. I'm going to hang up now. Take care, Miguel."

"Wait, no! Elsa! Elsa? Fuck! Fuck, fuck, fuck, fuck!"

16 THE DEPARTURE

One day passed. Elsa might not have been angry anymore. "Hey can we talk?" No reply. It was probably best to give her some time and space.

Five days passed. She would have travelled to Dubai by now. "Hey how are you?" Still no reply. This was strange.

Nine days. She might have seen her first manta ray already. "Hey I hope you're enjoying The Maldives!" Nothing. Maybe she'd lost her phone, or maybe she was ghosting him.

Thirteen. A concise and polite but non-apologetic reply very early on Sunday morning: She was flying back that day. She was fine. The Maldives had been spectacular, especially the manta rays! And she was always happy to talk, but she would be very busy for the next few days.

Up until now, Miguel had avoided getting Maria mixed up in this drama, but now he really needed her advice. He knocked on her door—on Hugo's bedroom door—but she had left about an hour ago to receive Elsa back at home. Hugo offered some advice in Maria's stead: to figure out, before it was too late, whether he was ready to take the plunge. Miguel didn't know what plunge he was referring to, so Hugo guessed he wasn't ready yet.

Miguel called Elsa, but she didn't pick up. She was starting work on Wednesday, flying on Tuesday, probably packing on Monday, and looks like spending quality time with Maria tonight. Miguel knew he wouldn't have much time, but much time for what?

Elsa saw Miguel's missed call but decided to ignore it. However, a few hours later, on Maria's insistence (and in line with her own unconscious longing), she decided to call him back. In their brief but polite conversation, she agreed to meet him the following evening once she was finished with her packing. Maria was pleased to have Elsa all to herself for the rest of the day but also to have aided in her and Miguel's reunion and, inshallah, reconciliation.

The next day around sundown Miguel headed over to meet Elsa at what would soon cease to be her local pub The Masons Arms.

He felt stuck going into the meeting because he hadn't been able to figure out what he wanted, only what he didn't want—namely, in descending order of confidence: one, he didn't want to (and couldn't even if he wanted to) stop Elsa from leaving London; two, he didn't want to move abroad for any girl; and three, he couldn't convince himself (and neither would he have been able to convince her) that a long-distance relationship would be fruitful. Thus there was only one thing he knew for sure he wanted as he sprayed three pumps of cologne and packed three condoms in his pocket before heading out to meet her.

Similarly, Elsa didn't know what she wanted from the meeting—she hadn't allowed herself the luxury of exploring it—but there was only one thing she knew for sure she didn't want: to hurt Miguel unnecessarily. To that end, she had recurrently gone through the process of identifying potential arguments and figuring out the best way to defuse them, such that by the time she closed her front door, she was confident she would be able to avoid any big blow-ups.

(Running through this mental exercise had also had the added benefit of suppressing the waves of nauseating affection that had afflicted her in increasing frequency as she packed, as she shaved her legs in the shower, and as she sent him the message letting him know that she was ready to meet now.)

Elsa was in rude health, and Miguel was instantly taken aback by her holiday radiance. Her sun-blushed skin, an asymmetric new hairstyle, and a strangely mature demeanour all added to the impression of abundant confidence. His nerves scarcely let him speak without first clearing his throat. He went through the predictable topics of conversation—her new appearance, her recent holiday, her imminent move—not quite perfunctorily but certainly only as a means to contain his raging interior forces. But he could only keep that up for so long because his incapacitating desire to consume her, unless expressed, was threatening to consume him instead.

"You know, Elsa, I look at you now, and I see the woman that you are, and I wish I could have been a fly on the wall throughout your childhood, to have been there every day to watch you grow into who you are today."

"That's either extremely sweet or incredibly creepy."

"Haha! No, I didn't mean to come across as a creeper."

"I know. I was just teasing."

A solemn pause, then a sudden thought, then a scary question: "Do you ever think much about the past?"

"I try not to. I have some fond memories that I like to revisit every once in a while. And I've learnt some lessons which I never want to forget. But, for the most part, I try to focus on my present self—without stealing from my future self, if that makes sense. Why do you ask?"

"Just wondering... How come you never talk about your previous relationships."

"What do you mean?"

"Well, the first time we spoke on the phone, you asked me about my previous relationship, but you asked me not to return the question. And the two times after that when I've tried to bring it up, you've avoided talking about it."

"I don't like talking about it."

"Clearly. But why?"

She intercepted a soft sadness seeping through her body. She gently gathered it and guided it to one side so that the rest of her thoughts could continue undeterred. "Because I read an article in a women's magazine that warned me against talking about past relationships with any man, except with my GBF—and you're not my GBF, are you?"

"Stop being silly and tell me about your most recent relationship."

No one could say she hadn't tried. "Not tonight."

"Not tonight? There may not be another night."

"Well, then even more reason why to spare that unpleasant conversation."

"But I want to know."

"And why do you want to know?"

"Because I'm trying to get to know you. How else are we to understand one another?"

"Not everything in life is meant to be understood."

"Why don't you just tell me?"

"Look, you're being pushy again. And I really don't think I owe it to you to tell you the story of why my ex-boyfriend committed suicide."

"Oh, I didn't know..." He contemplated an apology,

but he knew better than to expect it to alter the immediate course of events.

"Well, now you know. Shall we?"

And just like that, their last meeting in London was over. Outside the pub, Miguel asked if he could walk her home, but she didn't think that would be necessary. A dispassionate hug, a remorseful glance, and that was that: Elsa's back, Elsa's gait, Elsa's gone.

All he could think of was—no, he wasn't yet ready to verbalise that emotion, that drive, that universal condition which makes us humans unique among known life. So instead he began to physicalise it.

He could gallantly run after her. He might catch up with her just as she was turning the key in her front door. He could kiss her right there and then, a last-ditched attempt to overcome her inhibitions and conquer her affections. That way he would make her his, and he would make her feel desired like never before.

A ridiculous notion.

He would not be chasing after her. He would not be catching up to her just as she was entering her house. He would not be kissing her underneath the front door canopy, ripping their clothes off as they stumbled inside, ordering her to lie on her bed and touch herself. He would not be towering over her naked body spread out for him, imposing penis erect for her, gazing at the hypnotic ellipses drawn by her fast fingers, following her tempo on himself. He would not be telling her to stop, to lick her glazed fingers, to let him do the rest.

And he would not have the pleasure of going down on her to breathe in that alluring smell, of looking up to see her flush with anticipation, of sucking on her clit, of drawing little circles around it—first clockwise, then anticlockwise, then figures of eight—of running his tongue between her labia, of parting them and pushing his tongue deep inside her, of opening his jaw wider to push his tongue even deeper, of wanting time to end right then, of part-wishing for life to end in there, of giving in to his survival instinct and coming out to gasp for precious air, of telling her how good it tastes and how much he fantasises about that taste every fucking day, of gathering her arousal fluid with his middle and index finger, of swirling these lubed finger pads on her clit mimicking the patterns and rhythms she'd employed just a few minutes ago, of being told she's getting close, of being yanked by the back of his head towards her, of getting motivated by her hip gyrations and loudening moans, of sliding his middle and ring finger inside her, of arching them into a hook to locate and apply pressure on that ridged inner surface, of telling her this is it, he wants her to come in his mouth, of vibrating his head and whisking his hand, of being told not to stop, of being told she's coming, she's coming, of experiencing that pyrotechnic display of her innermost energies, of getting trapped between her thighs, of being forced to ride her pelvic spasms, of being released, of smiling at his accomplishment: her first orgasm, of watching her glistening ejaculate slowly trickle from her mildly engorged pussy to her gently dilated anus, of gathering it with his tongue, of eliciting a sensation so intense she had to push his face away. He would not have the pleasure of any of that.

And it was a shame, for he would have wanted nothing more than to continue to spoil her body, to glide his tongue along her inner thigh, to kiss and bite her calf, to suck on

her toes one by one while looking into her eyes, to stroke
his dick while staring at her gleaming pussy looking so
primed and ready now, especially with her hips swaying in
that way, to yank her by her ankles towards him, to lay his
dick on her belly, its base on her gold pubic triangle, its
head past her belly button, to see those subtle abdominal
lines form and fade as her core twitches with thrill, to ask
her how much dick she wants, to hear her say she wants it
all, to let her spit in the palm of her dominant hand and
evenly spread her saliva all over his dick, to let her grab him
by the shaft and guide him, to feel her moisten the tip by
running it up and down the opening of her vagina, to feel
her dip it in little by little before allowing the rest of it inside
her, to sink his dick all the way in, to watch it come out
glistening, to notice her watching the same with awe, to hear
her moans, to swallow her moans, to be told how good he
feels inside, to whisper to her in Spanish, to feel her
reaction, to do it some more, to feel her getting close again,
to grab her by the throat, to squeeze and hold and fuck her
hard and fast until her face hints the colour of Rioja, to
release her, to hear her gasp for air, to kiss her reassuringly,
to let her catch her breath, to squeeze again, to fuck her his
hardest this time, to hear her scream out a second orgasm,
to attempt to suck her tongue out of her mouth, to release
her, to let her gasp for survival, to be smothered by an
onslaught of muscular contractions—vaginal, thoracic,
appendicular—to be taken past the point of no return, to
tell her he's about to come, to hear her say she wants to
taste it, to pull out and rush to her face, to gaze at that face—
eyes transfixed, mandibles parted, tongue protracted—
begging him to come for her, to have that sight imprinted
in his mind for many years to come, to suddenly feel her

palm cup his scrotum and her fingers press hard against his perineum, to irrepressibly shoot his load while letting out an uncontrollable roar, to open his eyes and see his ejaculate all over her satisfied face, to watch her meticulously collect it with her fingers and transfer it to her mouth, to have that motion imprinted in his mind for the rest of his life, to watch her swallow it, to hear her say how good it tastes, to have her squeeze and suck any remaining drops from him, to be thanked for the nourishment, to be told to lie on his back, to have her lie on his chest, to listen to those last dying moans, to feel like a king next to his queen—fearless, hopeful, content—to be blessed by a shimmering shower of oxytocin and prolactin and serotonin, to love (and feel loved).

At a loss, he went back inside the pub and ordered another lager. He stared at it in pain. He felt alone, alone, abandoned. A human soul in London is like a beer bubble inside a pint.

The next day Elsa took a one-way flight to Stockholm.

17 THE SURPRISE

November was on the brink of December, and Miguel was getting increasingly irritated at his inability to move on from Elsa. He reckoned he should have moved on already. After all, she was out of his life now, and there was nothing he could do to bring her back. He tried fucking other girls, but the first time he was too inebriated to get it up, and the second time he felt dirty and repulsed after. And work, far from distracting him, only made things worse; his biggest commission around that time was a series of editorial portraits on the husbands of female military personnel who would be stationed overseas during Christmas, and this only got him thinking about long-distance relationships.

He decided to call her. He found her on Facebook Messenger—he had deleted her number—then tapped the phone icon. But he hung up before it rang; his gut forced him to. He analysed his nerves and concluded they were just an ordinary fear of rejection. He decided finally to be brave and call again. But, what if his real fear was of not calling, of conceding defeat? Thus he decided, really finally, to leave her alone and let her move on. Unless, what if this last thought was a symptom of self-loathing? That might explain why at times he'd felt undeserving of her love, like right after they had sex... He didn't want to think anymore. He was too confused now. The final, no, the ultimate decision to call or not to call would be postponed until a time when his head didn't ache as much.

Then, unexpectedly, he had the rarest idea: to call his sister. And this time he would not allow himself even the slightest pause for hesitation. Unfortunately, he couldn't find her number. (He didn't have it; he had deleted it many years ago.) Nevertheless, he did manage to find an old email address for her and send her a message that partially assuaged his anxiety. And she replied within a few hours.

Christmas (and his birthday three days later) was his least favourite time of the year. In recent years, he had escaped the commercial and familial conventions by backpacking in Latin America. This year, he was travelling to Switzerland to spend it (and his thirtieth) with Vanessa, his sister. This would be one of a handful of times he'd seen her since she moved out of his mother's home when he was fourteen, and the first time they had communicated in any way since her unreturned wedding invitation seven years ago.

Lausanne was a dreamy affair—strange but not altogether unfamiliar. Miguel took away something from his consanguineous reunion, but that something he would not be able to recognise, let alone verbalise, for several months. In fact, his drunken new year's resolution to fly to Sweden to see Elsa was, in his mind, completely unrelated to the influence his sister had begun to cast on him.

It was 5:25pm in Stockholm and Miguel was waiting in a coffee shop across the street from the entrance to Elsa's office. He'd been there a couple of hours, since sunset, patiently sipping peppermint tea and nervously scoffing cinnamon buns. He hadn't told her he was coming because he wanted to surprise her. And he had it on good authority—a bogus phone call and a leaky secretary—that she would be working that day. But a randomly overheard benign conversation planted in his mind the insidious idea that he might fail to spot her—if he hadn't already—thanks to the winter darkness and his frequently interrupted line of sight. So with that anxious thought, he hurried out of the coffee shop and walked over to the front door of her office building. And there he waited, rehearsing his lines in his head, blowing steam into his cold hands, and watching a thinning trickle of people exiting that door—none of them Elsa.

There's a popular saying in Sweden (and probably other Nordic countries too): 'There's no such thing as bad weather, only bad clothes.' Well, it's not entirely accurate. Yes, there exists bad clothing—Miguel would attest to that—but the other point is contestable, and even the most hardened Swedes would have scowled at the weather forecast for that week.

Miguel lasted until 5:45pm before he capitulated and sought shelter inside her office building. He would be fine as long as the reception was being staffed by the same or a similarly gullible secretary. In fact, he might even be able to enlist her in a masterly ploy to lure Elsa out. But the intercom was unanswered, the navy blue birchwood door was immovable, and his shy employment of the solid brass door knocker was ineffectual. His heart sank. He paused, to think. He turned around to see if anyone might be watching him with suspicion. He was safe. He took a deep breath to gather enough confidence to face the door again and knock harder. He lifted the door knocker up—it felt even heavier than the first time—to the horizontal and paused for a few seconds to try to estimate the speed with which he would have to push it to achieve the necessary loudness. When those seconds threatened to unite into a minute, he closed his eyes, made a wish, and let it free fall. And when he opened his eyes, he saw Elsa.

She was speechless. He was not. He told her he loved her, that he was in love with her in a way he'd never even thought possible, that he'd never met anyone like her, not even close, that she was rich—not rich like Bill Gates, but rich like the island of Australia, naturally abundant in everything that a man could ever need. This last one came out strange, and it made her laugh, but the point was this: he was willing to move to Stockholm to be closer to her, to be with her—if she would have him.

"I don't wish to undermine your revelation, but I don't believe you're in love with me."

He insisted that he was. He was sure of it.

"I believe that a series of events might have led you to a point where you felt vulnerable and that you've spun this narrative to try to deal with that emotion—but that's not love."

"What?"

"I suspect you're struggling to find a replacement for the function that I served. But you should try to understand that... that vacancy before you try to fill it." She didn't want to use the word 'void'.

"I'm not afraid of being alone."

"All humans are afraid of being alone. Those who don't feel it probably—"

"Elsa, I know myself. I know what I want: I want you. I'm here, aren't I? Standing right in front of you, in the freezing cold. And I've just told you that I'm willing to move to Stockholm for you. What more do you need me to do to prove it to you? What, you want me to get down on one knee?"

"Please don't."

"I wasn't going to. I was being sarcastic."

"Look, even if what you say you feel is true—and let's suppose that it is—love is only a part of it. There's much more to it than that, and I'm not sure you possess the tools to be with someone in the way you seem to be suggesting to be with me."

His puckered brows suggested that either he didn't understand what she meant or he didn't approve of it.

"I don't think I know how to say this without hurting your feelings, especially given the situation we find ourselves in."

"I don't need your protection. Just give it to me straight."

"Fine. I don't think you have the emotional capacity to satisfy me. You're somewhat... emotionally selfish, unwilling to give. Or maybe you're just empty, unable to give. I don't know. Either way, the upshot for me would be the same: I wouldn't receive all the support I would expect from the... from the—"

"Learning and growing—isn't that what life is all about?"

"Miguel, you're going to have to learn and grow by yourself, or at least without me, because I can't afford to take on another project right now. I've got too much going on."

"You call me selfish, but you're the one who's being selfish. And short-sighted! You're only thinking about your present self."

"Trust me. I'm really not."

"Think about the future we could have together!"

"I am thinking about the future."

"I don't understand. This isn't like you. I know that you have or at least had feelings for me. I know it! I felt it! So what's changed?"

"Look, Miguel, I really don't want to argue."

"And you think I flew all the way out here to argue?"

"No. So can we just leave it at that?"

"Leave it at that?" He sank into defeat drawing a dispirited sigh on his way down.

"Please don't be sad."

"I wish you could see things from my perspective." With that, as if prompted by his own words, he looked at Elsa, thinking this might be his last time. And from his perspective, she was clearly uncomfortable. She was avoiding his eyes, biting her lips, and gripping her forearms tightly across her middle. He hated the thought of this being his last memory of her, but he didn't know what else he could say to change her position. Where had he gone wrong? What had he miscalculated? Had he actually calculated anything, or had he just acted on blind impulse—or fear, as Elsa described it? Why had he imposed himself on her like this? Why hadn't he called or messaged beforehand to let her know his intentions? Had he known she would have talked him out of it? Miguel became trapped in spiralling rumination.

And so the silence grew between them until it started to snow again. Flocks of white particles swirled inside light cones underneath comforting luminaires. A flake of ice landed on Elsa's lip. She licked it and grew optimistic. She looked into his eyes. "Miguel, I have to tell you something."

"What is it?"

The Surprise

"I'm pregnant."

18 INNER CONFLICT

"I didn't want her to keep it and I told her so but she told me she was keeping it so that's why I left."

"Given your childhood, I can understand why your first impulse would be to run away."

"What?"

"Your father—he let you down. And now you're scared of becoming him."

"He was your father too. And he let us all down."

"I know…"

"So what do I do now?"

"Try to listen to your heart."

"How?"

"Pray or meditate or try to figure out what works for you."

* * *

Miguel had been unburdening to Vanessa via WhatsApp since hearing the bad news. And as a consequence, his relationship with her was continually strengthening. By contrast, his friendship with Hugo was beginning to wilt.

* * *

"I think I need a change of scenery. I'm getting fed up with London."

"How are things with your friend Hugo?"

"He's too far up Maria's arse to even notice anyone else, including me."

"It sounds like he's been bitten by the love bug."

"Yeah, well, you know I've always hated bugs. And it makes me sick to the stomach to see him like this."

"But I'm sure he still cares about you and would want to know what you're going through."

* * *

Miguel thought that he was merely concerned about his best friend's apparent loss of independence, but truth be told he was just jealous, jealous that Hugo seemed to have found happiness, that seemingly fraudulent over-the-top happiness that could only be seen on TV, among the members of the families in those milk commercials.

And Hugo did know what Miguel was going through. After letting the cat out of the bag, Elsa had rushed to tell Maria to avoid her finding out from Miguel via Hugo. Hugo wished he hadn't found out—he even got almost angry at Maria for telling him—because he knew he would have to hide it from Miguel as he would consider that an invasion of his privacy, something which in the past he'd never taken lightly (with other people that is, since Hugo had never invaded his privacy before). Besides, Hugo thought and cautiously argued that Miguel should be given a chance to open up in his own time. Alas, a few weeks into February, Hugo was still waiting for that time. Of course, Maria was done waiting by then, and she advised her man not to hold his breath, but he remained loyal and hopeful to his friend. Although holding in what he knew only added to the waves of foreign energies that Miguel kept perceiving from him.

* * *

"How could she do this to me?"

"You feel betrayed."

"How else would I feel? I mean, how could she just decide unilaterally on something that could affect my life so much?"

"You need to understand that her decision regarding her pregnancy was not about you. It was about her body and her future baby, so don't take it personally."

"But shouldn't I get to have a say in it?"

"And don't forget that she also rejected you."

"Yeah, thanks for the reminder."

"I only bring it up because it would be easy for anyone in your position to conflate the emotional response from both events: the rejection and the pregnancy. They're linked but they're separate—if you know what I mean."

"Yeah, I hear what you're saying. But I already have a pretty good idea of how I feel about both: I don't want to be a father and I certainly don't want to be with her after this."

"Did you try to explain to her the full extent of your feelings towards fatherhood, the whole thing?"

"No, I didn't. Maybe I should have? You think I should? But what if I contact her and she doesn't want anything to do with me?"

"Miguel, I think it might be a good idea to open a line of communication and, once established, to try to be as open and honest with her as you can. But I want you to be aware and wary of any verbal rumination that starts with 'I should have' or 'What if' because those thoughts will usually lead to nowhere— and they will exhaust you along the way."

"Yes, you're right... Okay, I'll have a think about what you said, about re-establishing communications and opening up and that."

"Good."

* * *

Things didn't improve for Miguel. A day after Valentine's Day, Hugo told him he was moving in with Maria, effective immediately.

"Whatever, you two practically lived together already."

"Do you have anyone you'd like to share the house with? Otherwise I'll schedule some viewings."

"Go ahead and schedule away."

"Well, ideally I'd like you to be there for the viewings."

"What for?"

"You know, to meet the viewers. After all, you're the

one who's gonna be living with them."

"Are you gonna take Elsa's room?"

"What? No, I will sleep in Maria's room—with Maria."

"So what's gonna happen to Elsa's room?"

"Elsa's old room will become a..."

"A guest room?"

"No, actually we're thinking of getting rid of the double bed and turning it into a... a study, of sorts." He knew full well now wasn't a good time to have a hypothetical conversation about kids down the line.

"Well, if you're leaving this house, I guess I should leave too."

Hugo took a couple of beats to compose his response: "I don't know whether to feel flattered as your friend or offended as your landlord."

"Nah, I've been thinking about getting a place of my own for some time. A studio. It makes sense now that I've got enough work coming in that I can justify it. Actually, I might even save some money overall if I let go of my shared studio space. This is just the push I needed."

"Oh, well then yeah, I suppose that makes sense. Whatever you want, bro."

"Good. I've had my eye on a few spots for a while. I'll make some calls. I'm sure one of them will work out, so expect me out of here by the end of the month."

"This month?"

He kissed his teeth. "March."

"Oh, okay."

* * *

"Maybe I should propose to her and try make a nuclear family."

"Is that what you really want?"

"I don't know what I want anymore... But that seems like

the proper thing to do, no?"

"If you weren't contemplating proposing to her before you found out she was pregnant, then I wouldn't recommend you contemplate it now."

"You're right. I'm sorry. What a stupid thought. Anyway, she would never agree to it."

"Don't apologise. Just be patient and keep listening to your heart. It will guide you to your answer, eventually."

* * *

Miguel hadn't had his eyes on a few spots for a while. And he wasn't going to make any calls. Instead, he randomly started looking for a second job, something structured to keep him occupied (distracted). He ended up getting a part-time gig as a waiter in a fancy cocktail bar. Minimum wage notwithstanding, the repetitive nature of filling and collecting empty glasses combined with the potential for picking up women appealed to him enough to keep him from quitting during those five hours a night, five nights a week. And okay, so he didn't know off the top of his head the recipes of any of their cocktails—Sex on the Beach, Sex and the City, Sex with an Alligator, etcetera—but all the ingredients were listed on the printed menus, and he could read.

And he was attractive. Good lord, it never seized to amaze him just how promiscuous women are when drunk.[11] He fucked as many of them as he could. By mid-March he had a core group of five that he regularly slept with, and by the end of March he had moved out of Hugo's house—like he said he would—and was living out of his

---

[11] Not only does alcohol lower inhibitions, but in women, it also massively increases testosterone (the main libido hormone).

rucksack, arbitrarily crashing at the homes of his top three (in ascending order): third, the one that made the best dinners; second, the one that had the most comfortable bed; and first, the one that bore the closest resemblance to Elsa.

* * *

"Do you think humans are a monogamous species?"

"I think we can choose to live and die in accordance to whatever principles we hold most dear. Why? What's brought this up?"

"I don't think it's the natural state for us humans — or at least for us men."

"Even if that were the case, there are many things that aren't natural — but we do them anyway because they're in line with our overarching principles. And I really don't think it's that hard, even for men. In fact, let me send you something, a meme I came across the other day, a quote by a man, one of those guru types. One sec... Found it! 'Monogamy is like when you find your favourite brand of beer or your favourite curry — you like it so much that you don't want to have any other!'"

* * *

Coincidentally, Hugo had once told Miguel that same quote. He said he'd first heard it from a Buddhist monk in the mountains of Thailand. The thought of a bold monk in orange garments giving anyone relationship advice had made Miguel chuckle then, and it made him smile now. So he decided to call Hugo. He missed their smoking sessions with their long talks about conspiracy theories, and psychoanalysis, and cosmology, and whatever else the THC would unearth. It had been too long since they'd spent some quality time together. In fact, they hadn't seen each other since Hugo had moved in with Maria. Miguel had been ignoring all his calls and rejecting all his invitations.

Hugo missed Miguel's call, and by the time he returned it Miguel's reconciliatory mood had waned somewhat. (In that short two-hour gap, an Instagram story by one of his top three (the most-comfortable-bed one) had pissed him off. It was only a Boomerang of her with her girls having fun on holiday, but it strongly hinted at the prospect of her being just fine without him.) So Miguel spitefully proposed to his old friend a game of tennis in Paddington Rec.

At first, Hugo was pleasantly surprised at the suggestion because he'd never managed to get him to agree to the same back when they lived together no more than a short walk from the outdoor tennis courts. But the more he thought about it after, the more he got the feeling that the match would be cancelled at the last minute—most likely an April showers' rain check or, if the weather held up, some unforeseeable but unavoidable work assignment.

However, Miguel had no intention of cancelling as he was nearing the point at which the marginal cost of continuing to avoid him would become intractable, and the last thing he wanted was an even more uncomfortable conversation down the line—like an intervention or something. No, seeing Hugo now and on his own terms was better; he would be more in control this way. And the outdoor tennis court would shelter him from Hugo's sly intentions because there is no way he would dare shout all his prying questions from across the court. It was the perfect plan. The least intimate setting imaginable.

Especially doubles. That's right, Miguel forgot to mention that he had invited two friends to come along: the one that made the best dinners and a bubbly friend of hers—single of course, how else. Hugo couldn't believe his eyes when he saw the three of them casually strolling into the tennis court fifteen minutes late, Miguel in the rear with a fat L dangling between his lips. Passive-aggressiveness at its finest. At least the girls could half-play, which is far more than could be said about stoned Miguel, who struggled just to hit the ball over the net and into his opponents' outer rectangle.

The instigator of this mess initially arranged the teams into a predictable boy-girl versus boy-girl. He proved more a liability than an asset to his teammate, so the game was totally unbalanced. But he didn't seem too bothered; he seemed to be having a good enough time groping her at every opportunity. Hugo's team won comfortably in straight games. For the second set, Hugo rearranged the teams into boys versus girls. It was much more balanced now, but the boys eventually lost five games to three. Hugo's slice serves and early volleys weren't enough to compensate for Miguel's unique uselessness.

After the game, the one that made the best dinners invited Hugo to join the three of them back at hers for some food and drinks. Hugo thanked her for the invitation but politely declined, making sure to drop the words 'my girlfriend' in the explanation. Miguel didn't like that gesture and mocked him childishly for it in front of the girls who didn't laugh.

* * *

"Vane, I think I hate her…"

"Hate is a strong word. But if that's how you really feel towards her, then that can be useful for you to know because acknowledging your feelings is the first step towards addressing them."

"I didn't ask for this shit. And she defo didn't seem like the type to wanna get preggers, let alone to wanna keep it."

"We don't know her story. She may have had a good reason

for her decision."

"What good reason could she have?"

"Without talking to her, we will never know her reasons for wanting to have this baby, and she will never know your reasons for not wanting to be a father."

"Maybe I didn't really know her."

"Miguel, have you tried contacting her like we discussed?"

"I wonder if she knows the sex yet... And what baby names she's got in mind... What do you think he or she will look like?"

"My little brother, that curiosity unless fed will never go away."

* * *

May had already replaced April by the time Miguel asked Hugo to meet again. Miguel felt bad at not having spoken to him since their tennis match, and also at having missed his birthday. But more importantly, the 2oz that he'd picked up from him last time had just run out.

Hugo agreed to meet on the condition that they meet alone. (He did not want to walk into a surprise double date again, not when he had a good woman at home.) Miguel was irked by the fact that Hugo felt he had the power to impose conditions over him, but whatever, his plan was just to buy his weed and bounce. However, their meeting would not go as Miguel planned, because Hugo had plans of his own. First, the weed was out of the question; Miguel would not be getting any more from him until he fixed up. Second, and most crucially, he was going to get some things off his chest; Miguel's immature and irresponsible behaviour was inexcusable given that Elsa was seven months pregnant with his son.

* * *

"Vane, my head is throbbing. I have a storm of thoughts thrashing around. I can't even think."

"Are you feeling ill?"

"And my heart is constantly jumping out of my chest. No, I'm not ill. But I feel like I'm losing myself."

"You need to anchor yourself. Get a routine going again. Why did you quit your waitering job?"

"Because it was menial slavery."

"Okay, fair enough. But maybe try to find something else also with regular hours, something a bit more fulfilling this time. And try to get a place of your own because your current living arrangement, crashing at friends' homes, isn't conducive to feeling anchored. And most of all, try to surround yourself with people you care about and who care about you… How's Hugo?"

"I don't even recognise him anymore. But then again, I don't recognise myself either."

"Explain."

"Nothing feels familiar. It's like I see myself in the third person doing the things I've always done, and I ask myself: 'Who is this impostor? Who is this person going around pretending to be me?' And I want to hurt him. I want to hurt him so bad, so he can wake up from his pathetic and insignificant existence. I want to crumble his facade. I want to break him."

"Miguel, this dissociation you're describing is a little bit concerning. You may need to seek medical help."

"Fuck that shit. Anyway, I gotta go or I'll be late. I'm meeting Hugo to pick something up."

"Try to remember what a good friend he's been to you over the years. Let him help you through this too."

"He's not the person he used to be. And I don't need his help. Goodnight."

"Miguel…"

* * *

Miguel threw the first punch—he hated finding out the gender from Hugo—a big swinging right—he thought it was the vilest and smuggest thing Hugo had ever done—Hugo ducked and dodged it—and he wanted to wipe the smug off his face and make him taste his own bile—and sprung back up, surprised that he had predicted Miguel's behaviour down to the way he would try to hit him first. That last-minute change from his glasses to his contacts was a wise move.

"Bro, calm the fuck down," said Hugo in a low volume voice but stressing each monosyllable as a warning. There was no one around this late on a weekday in this council estate residents' park, but any one of the flats facing it might hear and alert the police.

"Who the fuck do you think you are? You think you're better than me? You ain't shit!" said Miguel in a tragically manic voice before lunging at Hugo with everything he had and taking them both down onto the wet grass.

Miguel was on top of Hugo, unleashing a frenzied onslaught of punches towards his face, most of which were landing on his defensive elbows, but not all. Hugo still hadn't thrown a single punch. "Stop you fucking animal. Stop!" Just then one fist connected with his mouth. He felt his lip burst against his teeth, and he tasted iron. That was enough. He leaned into Miguel, threw both arms over his left shoulder, swung the left one behind his neck, the right one behind his arm and locked them both under his chin. He took a few hits pulling this move, but he now had him in an armlock.

"Fuck off and die!" screamed Miguel wasting the last of his breath.

Hugo tightened the armlock. He took some more hits to his left side from Miguel's right fist. (Miguel's left arm was now unusable inside the armlock.) Hugo couldn't believe the rage flowing through his best friend. Even at this point he didn't want to hurt him, but he had to neutralise him with an overwhelming show of power in order to defend himself. He wrung the armlock and pushed hard with his legs flipping Miguel over behind him. Now they sat facing away from each other, back-to-back like Gemini, joined by Miguel's neck and Hugo's arms. Inside this lock, Miguel could no longer hurt Hugo. "Are you gonna stop?!"

Miguel felt like he was going to pass out. He wanted out of that horrible lock. He tapped the ground three times.

Hugo didn't see or hear that. He squeezed one last time. He knew Miguel would be close to fainting. "Are you gonna fucking stop this shit right now?!"

With his right arm, Miguel searched for Hugo's left leg behind him, then tapped him three times. Then another three.

Hugo released, inhaled, exhaled. The sky was overcast, pink in the night, but it didn't look as if it would rain again.

After half a minute to a minute, Miguel had recovered enough of his breath to be able to throw Hugo a wicked smile. "I thought you wanted to kill me there," he said wryly.

"What's gotten into you?"

"Yo, I was just playing, big man. Chill."

"It didn't feel like you was just playing when you was throwing punches in my face."

"We're just two old friends scrapping it out, getting rid of excess energy. It's no biggie—it's healthy."

"Yeah, well, you got it out now?"

"Yeah, we're good. Like I said, I was just playing. I'm a lot tougher when I fight for real." That wicked smile surfaced again for a microsecond.

Hugo almost didn't see it. "I'm not interested in how tough you can get."

"Anyway, where were we? Oh, that's right, you were

lecturing me on how I should live my life and how I'm not a real man if I don't look after my son." And just like that Miguel threw the most vicious punch, raw rage in his eyes—and fear, three decades of accumulated fear. Hugo read the straight right, ducked down and left, coiled from the hip, and fired a mean left hook to Miguel's jaw.

Miguel woke up on his back under a light shower. The bitter rain against his face helped him regain consciousness. He propped his head up to look for Hugo so he could congratulate him on his fighting skills, but he was nowhere to be seen. He barfed and spat out some stomach acid mixed with blood. He put his hand on his jaw and opened it slowly. It was sore, and two of his molars were loose. He felt weak and faint again. Bright stars faded in and out his eyes, and a sharp tone rang faintly inside his ear. He leaned back to the position he'd just woken up from. He extended his arms and looked up at the sky and remembered all the times that his younger self had seen American child actors on TV make snow angels, and he remembered how jealous that had always made him feel. And for a split second, he made a promise to his unborn son that he would be there to make snow angels with him every winter of his childhood. But then the distracted part of him who disapproved of that thought caught the part of him who had thought it and bullied him into voiding the promise before it was valid, before it counted. (But not before the part of him who was observing all of this conflict from a distance heard it.)

* * *

"You awake?"

"Hey I just woke up. I was sleeping when you wrote. You're

up early—or very late—what's wrong?"

"I'm thinking of getting a vasectomy."

"What? Why?"

"Children suck."

"Miguel…"

"No, they really do. They suck the energy out of you. Time, money too. They suck individual dreams out of your soul and replace them with common goals. They suck the romance out of relationships. They suck and suck and suck and give nothing in return."

"Well, I'm not convinced by your argument. I've heard some non-parents jokingly speak that way, but never any parent— biological or adoptive. Quite the contrary, I've met many parents who said that parenthood tapped a previously unknown source of energy, that it opened the door to a better version of themselves."

"A better version of themselves? What version is that? The version with 2.1 kids and a semi-detached house on a mortgage and a family car with great mileage and enough space in the back for a golden retriever? No thanks. I don't want that version of myself. I don't want that life."

"You're focusing on the negatives."

"I'm not. Seriously, I just don't get it. Why would anyone sacrifice all their freedom just to be able to procreate, just to spread some DNA? The world's overpopulated anyway!"

"Miguel, you sound very upset. I'm not sure I can help you from here like this. Maybe it's best if you try to do something to de-stress. Maybe a little outdoor exercise?"

"I got enough exercise outdoors with Hugo last night."

"Oh, that's good! Are you guys hanging out again?"

"Anyway, I gotta go now. I'm late for a shoot. Talk to you soon."

"Miguel."

"What?"

"Please don't get a vasectomy."

* * *

Miguel wasn't really late for a photo shoot, but he was going to try to de-stress—in his own way. He left his shared studio in Westbourne Park, where he had crashed overnight because he'd wanted to be alone (or rather, because the only girl he'd felt like being next to, his favourite, the one who bore the closest resemblance to Elsa, had gone to bed early with her phone on silent (or really rather, because the only girl he ever really felt like being next to, the only one who really mattered to him, had left him a few months ago on a lonely night in Stockholm)), then went to the corner shop and bought a 35cl bottle of Tennessee whiskey. The Pakistani store owner—himself a victim of many scornful glances since arriving in England some thirty years ago—tried his best to conceal his judgment as he sold him the (40% alc. by vol.) liquor before 9am. But apparently his best wasn't good enough for Miguel, who promptly told him to go fuck himself.

Moving westwards along the canal, in the shadow of the Trellick Tower, Miguel drank two-thirds of the bottle as if it were ice tea before finding a cosy little spot against a yellow brick wall where he decided to sit down and get high. Once in position, he shifted a little to slide his hand into his usual weed pocket, and just then he remembered that he had none left. "Fuck!"

And this is where it began. His heart started playing up, kicking his ribs like never before. He put his right hand over it as if to beseech it to calm down. Nothing. He took a massive gulp of whiskey. Wrong move. It was like throwing fuel on a fire. And his heart started racing now, and he began hyperventilating, and his eyes and nasal cavities welled up, and muscles everywhere twitched, and hands trembled. And he was afraid, afraid, terrified! Fear, fear, panic!

It had been over nine years since his last panic attack, on Amanda's plane. And that was different. That was mild in comparison. This one embedded a physical violence, a muscular component to it that was alien to him. Miguel tried to count his breaths, naively hoping that would slow them down. And for a moment he managed to do it, or rather, he imagined himself managing to do it. Thus he summoned the courage to emerge from what had now become a quasi-foetal position. But he couldn't move. He was stuck. So he tried offering a deal to the panic attack, or to whoever it was that was controlling his body: "Let me move. Please let me move. Let me just get on with my morning before anyone sees me here like this, and we can forget all this ever happened. I promise." But the panic attack wasn't negotiating, and Miguel realised that he was trapped. And he was petrified.[12]

Miguel wholly believed that he would end in that instant, cease to exist, disappear from the history of humanity. Where was his sister? Would she cry if he went now? Probably, but he couldn't think of anyone else that would care. Maybe it wasn't such a bad moment to end, to fade to black, to go back to his mother... But, but what about his son?

---

[12] It's hard to explain the fear that can consume you when your body completely betrays you, when you're a prisoner inside your own shell. And neither would I want to, for this fear can never be explained so as to be understood but not felt. So I'll just say this: it's worse than being taken prisoner by the enemy—that at least you can avenge. But you really can't avenge your own body, not without sacrificing your true self.

The remainder of this psychotic episode was a multidimensional protraction of this indescribable fear. Counted in seconds, it lasted exactly—well, that's irrelevant really. Eventually, he unthawed and regained psychomotor control. Flaccidly he glided back to the studio and into a hidden pocket in his rucksack from where he took out a lone diazepam that a faithless part of him had long ago stashed away for this day. He stared at it dispassionately, made a secret wish, and threw it in the bin. Then he messaged his loving sister. Then he fell asleep inside the all-white infinity cove.

* * *

"She said I was emotionally selfish, unwilling to give, or empty, unable to give... It's hard to face the man in the mirror—but it's the only way forward for me from here on."

19 ACCEPTANCE

An early summer breeze was serenading London the day Miguel woke up having decided in his sleep to own up to his parental responsibilities. Overnight his consciousness had purged itself of all fear and embraced a new drive: a sincere will to live and to give life. His fear was dead now, killed during the birth of a new person. (Fear cannot survive outside of its host.) But the present Miguel was temporally and spatially connected to the previous Miguel. (That connection forms the nature of our identity.) Thus he hadn't discovered a new self; he had accepted a higher eventuality and, in the same stroke, as these things go, fulfilled that potentiality. Acceptance takes courage, and courage begets strength. And the dissociated I that had been timidly watching a reckless Miguel-vessel on a path of self-destruction during the past four months was strong again, strong enough to incorporate itself with all other I's into a cohesive singular I: Miguel. And Miguel felt whole again. And Miguel was bursting with ideas. And Miguel was full of hope. And Miguel was finally able to love. And Miguel would love his son wholeheartedly—and definitely better than Miguel's father, with all his secrets, had loved him.

The next step, contacting Elsa, came so easily that it made him chuckle at the aforementioned spatial and temporal connection. That previous Miguel seemed a parallel universe away now, and Elsa was unsuspiciously pleased about it. Although, in her typical Finnish fashion, she didn't express much emotion over the phone. But that's fine, because he just wanted her to hear the promise he had made to himself: that whatever happened he would be there for his son and be the best father he could.

Miguel also wishfully offered to travel to Stockholm to lend Elsa a helping hand in the weeks leading up to the birth—but she declined, of course. She wasn't angry at him or anything, but if she could manage eight months without him, she could manage the last one. He understood. This was all his doing. He had shattered her trust and crushed her opinion of him—and that might take months, maybe even years to repair. But he was ready for the long road ahead. Still, he definitely wanted to be there for the birth of his first child, and that was something that Elsa had no intention of stopping. She would never deny him that right—regardless of his initial, shall we say, trepidations about becoming a father.

Miguel's reunion with Elsa was, on hindsight, amusingly quaint. They met in Södermalm, in a healthy coffee shop specialising in Açai bowls. Miguel had the house special; Elsa, the peanut butter; and Aino, Elsa's mother and nominated birth partner and self-appointed chaperone for the occasion, the cocoa. They sat on a wooden deck table in the raised inner patio under the high noon sun. They spoke nothing of the recent past nor the distant future; they confined their pragmatic conversation to the baby's needs over the coming months. Miguel was on board with every point that Elsa raised, so she was able to move through her agenda swiftly. Meanwhile, Aino sat in silence thoroughly enjoying her cocoa Açai bowl. Her opinions, if she had any, were neither heard nor felt. And yet somehow, she produced a calming effect to the soon-to-be parents. The meeting lasted about half an hour. As they parted, Miguel thought he saw a hint of affection in Elsa's eyes. He had. There had been. Specifically, curbed optimism for her son potentially having a father in his life, and romantic nostalgia towards a man who, unbeknown to her, had placed her above every other woman he'd ever known.

After the meeting, Miguel walked down Hornsgatan the few hundred meters to his Airbnb apartment to write in his diary (a new habit) the following entry:

Wednesday 27 June 2018

Today I saw Elsa pregnant with our baby boy for the first time. I say 'baby boy' because he doesn't have a name yet. Elsa says she has a few ideas but doesn't want to say, because she'd rather wait until she sees him. She says she'll know once she sees him. And I felt him kick! Her stomach is absolutely humongous now, but I guess it's no longer big enough for him because he clearly wants to get out with those kicks. I can't wait to meet him. I also met Elsa's mum Aino. I got very good vibes from her. She's very wise—somehow I could sense it. I may read this back and think it's weird (I hope not!) but honestly it felt like she was radiating positive energy. Imagine a life devoted to personal development and spiritual growth (because that's what I think she's done). Imagine how much ~~knowledge~~ ~~experience~~ wisdom you could amass that way by the time you got to middle age. Anyway, I'm really pleased Aino is going to be with Elsa in the hospital room as her birth partner. With her there, I know everything will be alright!

Also, FML but I'm still in love with Elsa! Sigh. The old me might have been ashamed to admit it, but I can't deny it. It's true. The moment I laid eyes on her again I felt something inside my chest kick me harder than baby-boy-without-a-name kicked his mama. But I don't want to blab on about this because I don't think it's healthy for me to focus my energy on these types of thoughts. (I'm not planning on suppressing them, but I might just have to make space for them and get on with things because my love life is not a priority right now.) But still I think it would be useful for me to note this thought down—for future reference.

That was his last entry before his son was born three days later.

Miguel closed shut his Moleskin notepad, slid it back in his North Face rucksack, and headed out westwards towards Turnbull for no particular reason other than he hadn't walked that way before.

Along the way, his attention was yanked by a little ice cream shop and factory (one could see from the front door how the ice cream was being made) where a lone young man was experimenting with fresh dairy, random deserts, and liquid nitrogen. Miguel went inside and struck up a conversation with him. His name was Samuel, and he'd recently moved out there after graduating from uni in London to try to make a living out of his true passion—or one of them, at least. Miguel had a taste of Sam's culinary and philosophical concoctions and was instantly hooked. So much so that over the next two days, he went back there and shot a documentary—his first short film—of this remarkable young man and his fantastic ice cream recipes.

20 NATIVITY

It was just before 5am on Saturday morning when Miguel received the call from Aino. But it wasn't until he half woke up two hours later that he heard her voicemail. Elsa had gone into active labour, so they were moving to the hospital. He flew out of the apartment (forgetting to lock the door). He ran the 1.1km to Södersjukhuset hospital in 7min and made it to the main entrance by 7:11am. He asked for directions to the Birthing Centre. He jogged there. At the reception he was nervously told that Elsa had been transferred to the Labour Ward. He asked for directions. He power-walked there. At the reception he was impassively informed that Elsa was currently being operated on. He sat down and waited, and waited, and—

"Miguel... Miguel, can you hear me? Nod if you can hear me."

"I can hear you."

"Good. Tell me what you remember," said a man with all the mien of a hardened surgeon.

Miguel closed his eyes, and in a flash, a flood of unthinkable visions swept through his mind. He reopened them as a countermeasure, but then the room started spinning. He tried, unsuccessfully, to raise himself from the hospital bed he found himself in then shouted, or half-shouted, which was all he could muster: "Where's Elsa?"

"Miguel," said Aino who was standing to his left in front of a sky-filled window. Her silhouette gradually brightened and filled in with features until Miguel was able to identify her. She pressed her left palm reassuringly against his heart. "You're in pain," she said, "and that's okay."

"What pain?" Miguel thought. "That was all just a bad dream," he told himself. Then he looked at his arms, legs, torso, and surroundings as if baffled by it all.

"My name is Mr Lindqvist. I'm a senior obstetrician here at the hospital." And with his foot, he activated the electrical motors in the bed, slowly tilting Miguel into a more upright position. "I ordered to have you sedated because you suffered quite a violent reaction to the news I gave you a few hours ago."

"I want to see Elsa and the baby," Miguel demanded feebly.

Aino squeezed his hand in hers, and he felt her bravery flowing into him.

"I'm afraid there were some complications during labour," explained the surgeon. "Frankly, we were totally unprepared when we received the patient in cardiogenic shock. Our initial diagnosis was that the shock was caused by a pulmonary embolus. Statistically, this was the safest bet given that no family history of cardiac disease had been reported, and we had to act quickly because in these situations even seconds can be crucial for the survival of the mother and the baby. So we began to deliver the baby by caesarean and almost simultaneously to search for the embolus in the mother. We were able to deliver the baby healthy and unharmed, but our initial diagnosis for the shock had been erroneous; it actually turned out to be hypertrophic cardiomyopathy. However, we spotted it too late, and by that point and despite our best efforts we weren't able to treat the severe brain hypoxia... I'm sorry for your loss."

Miguel said nothing. He returned a blank stare devoid of any visible reaction save for a stray tear.

The surgeon walked away to give Miguel some time to assimilate the news. By the door, he turned to add that a psychologist was available and could be summoned if needed, but he decided not to after seeing Miguel crying softly in Aino's arms.

Aino checked Miguel out of the hospital and took him for a walk; she felt he could do with the fresh air (and the company). After enough walking, she took him to that Açai place for breakfast. Miguel wasn't hungry, but she still went ahead and ordered two matcha lattes and two cinnamon buns—a regular one for the new father and one with little cocoa nibs for herself.

Miguel asked to sit inside this time. It was a warm and sunny summer morning but enjoying the good weather didn't seem right; in fact, neither did talking, nor eating, nor being alive while Elsa—

Aino saw Miguel glaring at the leaf-tattooed foam in the cup resting between his hands. He was frowning as a flurry of fearsome thoughts were surely frothing in his head.

"Elsa told you that she wanted to have a look at the baby before settling on a name. But to be honest, she was almost settled. She wanted to name your son Manuel. Manuel Laine Mbele."

21 FUNERAL

Elsa's heart, liver, and kidneys weren't suitable for donation because they were severely damaged by oxygen deprivation from when she'd gone into shock. So they—along with her brain and general muscle tissue—went to Karolinska Institutet for first-year, first-term medical students to dissect. However, her lungs, pancreas, intestines, cord blood stem cells, blood, bone marrow, bones, tendons, skin, and corneas were all harvested for potential donation as per her registered wishes. So there really wasn't much left to bury or scatter.

Aino, Miguel, and baby Manuel landed in Vaasa, Western Finland on Tuesday. It was Manuel's first time ever on a plane—then again, everything for a while would be his first. The three of them were picked up from the airport by Elsa's father, Elias: a stoic old man in a trusty old Land Rover with a spanking new car seat. As the three of them grappled in turns to secure the baby to the middle seat in the rear (statistically the safest position in a car), Miguel was reminded of the duality of the events that took place in that frightful hospital ward. He clearly heard the words 'the principle of equivalent exchange' spoken in his head, strangely enough in his mother's voice, and he floundered between being frightened or comforted by it. But he settled on the latter as he wistfully conjured up a never-ending childhood hug from his sister.

Elias drove one hour north to his and Aino's home just outside the little town of Nykarleby in the Swedish-speaking region of Ostrobothnia. He drove the entire journey with the utmost precaution, so Miguel was surprised to see him unexpectedly slow down in the middle of an empty regional road and head into what looked like an unofficial clearing for making U-turns, but which proved to be the opening of a dirt road through a pine grove. The 4x4 handled the rough terrain with ease, and the baby seemed wholly unbothered by the bumpy ride. After a few minutes the trees parted, revealing the coast and a harbour. From spring to autumn the sea melts, so they had to reach the island by boat, Elias said. Manuel's first time ever on a boat—that thought again.

The log cabin came into view as the motorboat navigated around the small island. It was idyllic, just as he had imagined; the perfect place to unwind, just as Elsa had described. In the distance, Timon & Pumbaa eagerly jumped and barked by the mossy pier. But once the boat was moored, they were sad and quietened not to see Elsa as they'd been expecting. Nevertheless, they were still happy to receive their new guests, especially the baby, who they greeted and examined with astounding care. The pair solemnly escorted the humans to the house then trotted off into the sombre woods to convey the bad news to the pinnacling pine tree and mourn their loss together.

Miguel held back his tears as he entered the cabin. This home might originally have been constructed as a symbol of Family, and now it was unveiling everything he had unknowingly wished to emulate with Elsa. Until that harrowing thought caught up with him again. Then suddenly the house became vague, ambiguous, like an inkblot, ready to take on any meaning projected by its viewer—in Miguel's case, mortality.

After dinner—a traditional fish stew served on a plate of mashed potatoes and lingonberry jam—the three of them sat by the fireplace sipping on a single malt Scotch and listening to an early David Bowie vinyl. Miguel was pleased that Elsa's parents appreciated good music and fine whiskey. He could get used to them. For Christmas he would make sure to give them a bottle of The Quiet Man. It is peculiar that he was already thinking about spending Christmas with them, but he was drawn to their energy, and he was extremely thankful for all the support they were showing him and his son.

Miguel asked them to tell him about their life, starting with how they met. The pair harmoniously unfolded their past with a palpable tenderness. He was warmed by their love story, but he also felt somewhat envious at times because his one true love story—the story of how he met and fell in love with Elsa—had been so brief in comparison.

That night Miguel and his son slept in Elsa's room. It hadn't been redecorated in possibly decades and still contained some items from when she was just a little girl. Her parents gave him permission to go through her stuff if he wanted to. They didn't think she would mind given the circumstances and given the fact that it might help him to teach Manuel one day who his mother had been. But frankly Miguel wasn't ready for that; it was too much too soon. Her cork board photo wall haunted him the most. And that night, in Elsa's bed, Miguel almost drowned under an ocean of imagined memories of his abiding love.

And in their room down the corridor, as they

exchanged back massages before their regular bedtime meditation session, Elias and Aino had what they like to call an open-heart conversation. This was not a daily occurrence, and it would have been their most painful one to date had it not been for the baby's presence, which was permeating the house and their souls. In fact, the child had innocently taken on a new meaning: he had become an emblem of the never-ending circle of life. So they couldn't be angry at the universe. And they knew that their daughter's spirit was resting in peace. For they understood that if it came to it, they too would give up their lives for their child. Their only wish right now was that they might still be able to... But that was never going to happen. So they sat in a singular lotus position and meditated as one, unavailingly wishing that their unified energies might once again recreate that unique part of their shared experience on this earth which had defined them and bonded them beyond all measure. Then they lay down and gently escaped their temporal bodies on to the plane of eternal longings in search of her.

Miguel was sitting on the dock of the bay singing to his baby in the morning sun when Aino appeared with a cup in each hand. He drank the hot cocoa with pleasure and asked about Elias. She didn't know where he was, but she guessed he'd gone into the woods with the dogs.

Miguel and Aino were 80 pieces into a 1,000 piece jigsaw puzzle when Elias emerged from the woods accompanied by Timon & Pumbaa. Miguel was astounded by the physical presence that this almost octogenarian man who had just lost his daughter emanated. Elias asked Miguel to accompany him into town and Aino to look after

Manuel in the meantime. Both of them willingly obliged. Their jigsaw could wait.

Miguel had gathered by now that Elias and Aino led a private life, but he was still surprised to observe that the townsfolk were unaware of Elsa's passing. However, if her parents had decided to make her funeral small and intimate, then that was their prerogative. And frankly, Miguel agreed. After his mother died of cancer, he didn't arrange any grand old ceremony either.

On the drive back, Miguel thought he saw a moose behind a dense thicket along the side of the road. He had, and if he was really lucky he might also spot a wolf during his visit; there'd been a few sightings recently. Elias also let him know about the abundant sea trout in their cove in the spring, and he promised to take him spin fishing there one day.

Elias and Miguel returned to the cabin with all the food and drink for tonight's barbecue, including Elsa's favourite cake: strawberry gateau. Aino was happy to report that Manuel had been a good little boy and hadn't cried once. The four of them had lunch: formula for the baby and salad for the adults. After lunch, Elias got started on the marinade for the meats, and since he didn't need help, Miguel and Aino went back to their 1,000 piece puzzle. Soon after finishing up in the kitchen, Elias left to pick up the others from the airport. Miguel hadn't slept enough so Aino paused their jigsaw and asked if she could take the baby to keep her company in the workshop (thus freeing Miguel to take the nap she could tell he desperately needed).

Aino didn't get much work done. She couldn't help staring at Manuel—so tiny, innocent, vulnerable—and she couldn't stop her mind from swelling with flashbacks of Elsa during all stages of her life, from her birth to her giving birth. Aino knew she would never until the day she died be able to mend her broken heart, so rather than wastefully trying to fight the pain, she accepted her loss and wept, wept onto the block of wood that she was working on and into the latent rocking horse that would one day emerge from it.

Meanwhile, Elias was speeding past 130km/h on an 80km/h road, strangling a scream, foolishly trying to outrun the onslaught of thoughts that were cutting through his head when, suddenly, a moose flashed in front of him, and he lost control of the vehicle. Miraculously his seven-seater Defender didn't flip, and he safely skidded to a halt. But how could he ever hope to move forward from his loss. Finally he let out a wail of heartbreak and begged God for forgiveness, for strength and guidance, and for a reason to keep on living.

And in Elsa's room, Miguel is walking through a faint trail in a claustrophobic forest; the dense canopy above forcing a cool and damp climate on the ground; the shards of light cutting through the high foliage the only hints of a world beyond this one... He's holding a letter he wants to deliver, but his body is weary from endless walking, and he yearns for somewhere to rest and recover—like a clearing where he may bask in the sun and recharge his strength and devise a plan out of this dark forest... So he focuses his spirit and makes a single wish: "Please let me rest." And the trees, as if they've been listening to his thoughts but were unable to offer help until asked for it, grant him his wish and present to him an immaculate clearing. Thus Miguel realises that he is being listened to, that there are forces in this forest beyond his understanding but not entirely outside of his control... He enters this holy garden and sees, in its centre, illuminated by an angled shaft of bright sunlight, a dark sarsen stone—one metre high, two metres long, one metre wide—made out of lithified peppercorns. He is inexplicably drawn to it. Flaccidly he glides there. Now he's lying supine atop it. He closes his eyes and takes a deep breath: inhale, the peppercorns in the sarsen begin to shift underneath him; exhale, the sarsen begins to swallow him whole... Suddenly he realises he's entering his sarcophagus, but he isn't scared; he knows instinctively that he has the power to stop this if he so chooses. And yet he doesn't, he doesn't stop it. He accepts his fate as inescapable and sacrifices his entire person to the stone, to the forest, to time... Death.

When Miguel wakes up the cabin is empty, but through a window he sees a thin trail of smoke drifting into the dusking sky, and underneath it he sees a little mountain of firewood burning on the sandy shore, and to the side of it he sees a group huddled around Manuel—his newborn son. It looks like Elias and Aino, and Iida and Aada and Aku, and Vanessa, and Hugo and Maria, and Timon & Pumbaa. He smiles and waves at his new family but they don't see him. Then he starts walking towards them but they don't seem to notice him. Then, from afar, he overhears one of them say: "Wow, he looks just like Elsa!"

With special thanks to Sekemi Aderemi, Carl Walton, Izzy Podro, Stephen Whitmey, Dia Vadai, Audrey Borowski, Vanessa Ruiz, Tanja Nyholm, Hal Bilton, Sheila Ruiz, and Manuel Ruiz Quesada.

ABOUT THE AUTHOR

I'm just a guy...

SPILT PEPPERCORNS is my debut novel.

www.amosruiz.com